The Morrison Files

Touch
Me
Like You
Do

Book One

A.J. Marx

Everything was fine until that sexy and brilliant, blue-eyed Adonis, Shayne Matthews, walked onto the stage of the convention.

He wasn't even supposed to be here.

But from the second he opened his mouth and that sultry voice said my name, all I've done is daydream about what he looked like under those fancy dress clothes.

What's wrong with me? I'm not that kind of girl.

I'm a professional, I don't get distracted. And this speaking engagement was the next step in my career—I can't be going all gaga even if he was hotter than sin.

There's just something about him, something that tempts me to break all my rules.

All I had to do was say yes.

Contains mature subject matter, sexual content, 18+readers only.

E-book ISBN: 978-1-7753686-3-2
Paperback ISBN: 978-1-7753686-7-0

Written by A.J Marx
Proofed by Donna Sears
First Edition June 2019

Theo & Quinn Creative Works
Shediac River, New Brunswick, E4R 6A7, Canada

www.facebook.com/AJMarxAuthor/

To continue the journey click here:

https://www.amazon.com/A.J.-Marx/e/B07QDNTXGZ

To sign up for our newsletter go to
https://dl.bookfunnel.com/ps6yp54y7l
or ajmarxauthor@gmail.com to get the
latest updates and special offers from the author
herself.
Or follow her at
www.facebook.com/AJMarxAuthor/

Like to be part of the action?
Want to be more involved in my books?

I am always on the lookout for ARC
(Advanced Reader Copy) readers to help make the
stories come to life.

If you would like to receive early copies of
my books and love being part of a small team,
contact me here: or ajmarxauthor@gmail.com

This book is dedicated for all those who have felt that strange, and sometimes sudden, pull towards another—even when you're not able to put a finger on why but just know there is something deeper going on here that only your soul knows the reason why.

The Morrison Files

Touch
Me
Like You
Do

Book One

A.J. Marx

Chapter 1

I never knew it could be this way—never knew it was supposed to feel like this.

*

Turbulence was crazy as the plane touched down in Saint John's. The captain made an announcement over the loudspeaker, quite pleased that we had made a smooth and safe landing. The safe part was a given but if he thought that was smooth, I didn't want to know what a rough one was.

Gathering the hotel address out of my carry-on bag, I waited for my luggage to arrive in baggage claim—studying the map of the harbour on my phone and trying to figure out how far away the hotel was from here.

My eyes lifted in search for taxi signs and I moved in that direction once my stuff appeared on the conveyor belt. Airports always had an abundance of drivers, eagerly waiting to whisk the travelers off to their destinations. Not that this was unusual or anything but in my experience of traveling, there was always a wait. On more than one occasion I've seen a fight break-out between tired and unruly passengers desperately wanting to get somewhere, anywhere but the airport.

This morning there were no riots, and it wasn't too long before I hailed a cab and tucked inside, luggage in tow.

Giving my driver directions, I settled back into the stale smelling seat and took in the lights of the still darkened city, going over my notes for the presentation I would be giving later on that day.

This wasn't a huge conference. Only a few hundred of the higher ranking managers and assistants of the businesses would be attending. It's supposed to be a morality uplifting kind of weekend to refresh burned out minds in much need of a break.

And so I came.

Not as a burnout but as part of the panel. My speeches on self-worth and learning how to say no to negativity, caught the eye of some big wigs at the last small conference I had spoken at and they put in a request to have me attend as part of the roster two weeks later.

It wasn't the best offer I had received but when I heard that Warren. S. Matthews, world renowned self-made Billionaire, was to speak on his own journey to success. I jumped at the offer. He was someone I had always wanted to aspire to be like and his history of rags to riches was inspiring. Wanting to be at one of his events was a top runner on my bucket list.

So, for me, it was like killing two birds with one stone.

Getting paid to inspire and be inspired? Definitely, a no-brainer there.

And it was impeccable timing—a perfect opportunity to take a much-needed step back from my life.

Well, not my entire life. I was on a fast track to building a new career for myself—one that was more about becoming me—the real me. Not the one everyone expected me to be or thought I could only be.

I had had enough of working for everyone else and watching them follow their dreams while I stood in their shadows, barely grasping at straws to pay the bills. I decided it was my time to stop watching and start doing. And so became the new person I wanted to be, Andy Morrison, life coach, and inspirational speaker.

And, as it turned out...I was good at it.

Helping others with their lives, seeing what should and should not be allowed to take up space in their worlds—that part was easy-peasy.

It was my own life that needed a little help. Still struggling a bit on how to do that, was where it got hard.

Enter Jeremy.

Somewhat thoughtful, pretty easy to look at, sporty and well spoken, he was all that. What's not to love right? It's just that...well, even though theoretically he was in a relationship with me, I wasn't really sure if he is 'all in'. I barely saw him and when I did, maybe we would be intimate and maybe we wouldn't.

I know it's not all his fault.

It takes two.

And I know I had been traveling a lot, especially of late, but even when we were together, it was...well, let's just say it wasn't quite as magical as the fireworks display at Disney, nor was it an earth-shattering moment—one that made you long for the next and the next—dying for when you could be alone.

It was more like taking a lukewarm bath or being handed a few sparklers that fizzled out halfway down the stick to light up in the dark when everyone else was given rockets.

But he was sort of a good guy.

Good guys were safe and steady.

And safe and steady was...well, Jeremy.

Kind of.

The driver shoved the car into park and turned over his shoulder announcing our arrival—pulling me out of my melodramatic love life scenario and thrusting me back into the now.

"That'll be twenty even, love," he chimed over his shoulder with a coffee buzzed grin. His easy sweet words cradled my heart, saving it from my dampened mood, and forcing me to put on a smile as I hand him his money.

The day's first light drew my eye away from the cab as it drove away, revealing the city now painted with a rosy hue as it awakened before me.

"Need help with your bag Miss?"

The words shook me from my daydream and I turned to meet the cheery brown eyed bell boy. An optimistic smile tugged on my tired mouth. "Yes, that would be lovely, thank you."

He gathered up my two small travel bags hurrying toward the spinning doors of the Lexus Inn, and I turned away from the city to follow him in.

Standing at the edge of the lobby, I took in the hotels cleanliness and its pristine lure, eyeing the halls that I suspected led to the conference room that would be filled to the walls soon enough. Uniformed staff was busy setting up already, bodies hurrying to and fro, in and out of the opened doors, carrying all sorts of chairs and rolling in tables on trollies. All their faces drawn with lines for mouths, and stress-filled eyes, glancing time to time to the rather large man holding a clip board—busily scribbling notes and flipping sheets.

I smiled at them as they worked away, while I waited for my reservations to be confirmed in my sleepy state just as the same young bell boy with dark brown eyes approached me from the side.

"I'm sorry miss, but there's a bit of a mix up—and unfortunately, a small wait while they straighten up your room. They weren't expecting you until later, and somehow the rooms have gotten a little behind schedule. Busy exciting weekends tend to do that," he added with a sweet innocent smile, his eyes wearily watch my expression, probably hoping like hell I won't blast him for the mistake.

I granted him with a moment of peace, donating an understanding smile. "That's fine."

"The bar is open Miss if you'd like to wait in there. The seats are very comfortable and whatever you care to order, will, of course, be on the house for this unpleasant delay of your lodgings."

I smiled again, picking up my carry-on bag sitting at my feet. "That's fine, thank you."

"I will have someone come to gather you once we have this all straightened out, and have your luggage delivered to your room if you like."

"Thank you...that would be wonderful."

Not sure if it was the desperation in his voice or the tiredness of the flight kicking in but a visit to the bar for a little 'nightcap' or rather a 'morning cap' sounded good—followed by a nap if I was to be on my game come lecture time.

The young man ushered me into the bar and explained to the bartender the instructions for my billing. She only smiled at me but gave a quick roll of her eyes to the boy, shaking her head, which I caught but pretending I didn't, I slid into one of the high set chairs and ordered a mimosa.

What better way to start my stay than with a little champagne and some orange juice—breakfast of champions my friend Kimmie would say.

Chapter 2

After a couple glasses of bubbly juice, my fatigue from the early hour and the ride had caught up with me. My eyes heavy and my words slurred on my tongue. I didn't bother making small talk with the bartender as she looked just as tired. I leaned back into my seat and let the heaviness in my eyes have their way, closing them for a moment. Or what had seemed like a moment. A low gentle voice stirred me from my moment of silence.

My lids fluttered, trying to open to a tall thin young man hovering over me. "Miss Morrison?"

Straightening in my chair, I swallowed down the thickness in my tongue and spoke, "Yes?"

He smiled and tucked his hands behind his back. "Your room is ready."

Still caught in my fatigue, my legs felt sluggish as he escorted me to the front desk for a quick sign in and another apology, then it was off to the elevator.

I rode up to the top floor, leaning into the mirrored walls until the doors opened. Disembarking into the hallway, the floor resembled a more of an up-scaled version of the downstairs lobby. Chandeliers hung from the ceiling and elegantly placed lanterns lit the long slender corridors. I glanced down at my key, my eyes a bit unfocused from the earlier refreshments no doubt and headed towards the small gold sign that said Marilyn suit. "Hmm, sounds cozy," I said to no one, sauntering down the hall.

With a quick swipe of the card, I was in—eager to have a nice long shower and hopefully sneak in a nap before the midday presentations began downstairs. Mine wasn't until later this evening so in theory, I had plenty of time to liven up.

Pushing the door wide with my backside and backing into the room, I dropped my bags and stop dead in my tracks as I turned around. "What in the hell?"

This was no standard room with a little kitchenette like I had requested. Nope. Not even close. This was a large and luxurious suite, with all the fixings of an apartment. "This has to be a mistake," I say, thinking I can't afford this and rushed to the phone to call the front desk.

After a few moments of explanation of who I was and where I was, the debate was settled by a quick 'it was the only room available at the time of your arrival'.

"Is everything to your liking?"

"Ah, yes, quite."

"Wonderful, we hope you enjoy your stay. Please help yourself to the complimentary minibar."

My eyes shoot the larger than normal black fridge standing in the corner of the room as I slurred a quick thank you over the phone and slowly made my way towards the fridge. The last time I travelled, I took a bottle of beer and some other morsel of food because I had missed the hotel kitchen closing before I got back from my presentation, but this meager sustenance nearly cost as much as the room did.

I pulled on the handle, revealing the treasures inside and nearly fell over—a low whistle blew over my lips. There were two small bottles of Champagne, a limited selection of beer, wine, plus a few other fancy things that I wasn't sure of, but was willing to investigate later before I check out.

"Wow, now this is service. I hope I get screwed over more often."

Letting the door close behind me I headed for the shower. It's amazing what a quick warm rinse does for the soul. Slipping into the fuzzy white robe that was folded neatly on the bathroom counter, I wandered my way back into the room and folded back the freshly laundered sheets of my bed—fading into my dreams on the microfiber pillows, really loving this whole bucket list trip decision already.

So what if my love life sucked. Today, I have fluffy pillows, a fridge full of champagne, and a speaking engagement that could possibly be life changing. I will deal with my pitiful romantic drama later. Right now, was all about taking in the ambiance, raising my client's standards of themselves and letting this morning's mimosas slip me into a nice dreamless sleep.

Chapter 3

The rest of the morning slipped away uncontested under the spell of slumber. It was nice.

Too nice.

Something about it felt off—even my apartment wasn't this nice.

My eyes rushed open. The sting of panic jerked my head from the pillows, desperately seeking out a clock.

My hands rushed to pick up my cell on the nightstand, touching buttons to wake it up—Twelve Bells.

A loud exhale sounded. It's only noon. Letting go of my breath and I fell back into the pillow, closing my eyes—my mind settling back in search for the corners of the strangely provocative dream that had kept me quite happily asleep. But it failed. Unable to find the hard muscular imagery of the man I was engaging with, it grabbed hold of reality—thrusting me into a crowded room, thousands of eyes all on me. I lurched up out of bed revisiting the clock's face, flipping back the covers with a curse and rushed to the shower.

"Crap, crap, crap." I curse, ripping off the robe and jumping into the cold spray coming from the showerhead and letting out a high-pitched yelp.

I was going to be late for the first speaker.

Chapter 4

The conference room was filling up quickly as I casually weaved my way through the crowded room. The manager had left instructions with the front desk to inform guests who were attending the conference, where the reserved speaker tables were located. At the front of the room, along the edges, each table was decorated with small centrepieces—water, napkins, notepads and pens, and every spot was assigned with names to each of them.

With my coffee in hand, I heaved my bag, filled with notes over my shoulder and smiled—zigzagging through the room of buzzing bodies, happy to be away from their day jobs and just excited to be out, unhindered from their daily lives.

This was a good sign.

This would make my job so much easier but it was still a long way off before I would stand before them and speak. Things could change drastically, depending on the mood of the room, and who knows if their happy buzz boats would still be afloat by then.

I sat taking notes—each presentation delivered with precision and kept to script by a watchful timekeeper, who sat on the edge of the makeshift stage—elevated just enough so everyone in the room could see and hear. Only once, or twice, he had to approach the speakers—a warning sign for them to begin wrapping up their messages and clear the stage for the next speaker.

Brief intermissions in the middle of it all, were allotted to allow some movement and stretching of the legs. At least they had the brains enough to throw in that concept. The trick to keeping people focused and engaged was to allow them small breaks in the day for social interactions and necessary bodily functions to be performed. A presentation where random bodies being excused here and there, as innocent as it may seem, was still a disruption—conscious or not of this fact, it still affected everyone in the room.

The last intermission had served its purpose and the wave of boredom swept away momentarily, edging on the last of the day's lectures and my time had come. So late in the day and with people's attention spans were waning, a small wave of panic washed over me knowing my speech had better be spot on and ready to steal their attention back or my job and my dreams would be rendered mute.

I sat quietly going over all I had prepared in my head, checking, confirming points I wanted to cover. An older lady approached me from the back. "You're up in five minutes, Miss Morrison," she whispered quickly into the side of my ear, nearly scaring me out of my pants before tucking herself back against the wall, waiting for me to proceed onto the stage.

Closing my files and notes, tucking them neatly into their case, I set it down and rose from my chair. Pressing a wide smile on my lips I nodded to her in thanks and headed around the edge of the dark velvet curtains. A tiny dark haired girl standing in the shadows waved me over. Quickly sidling up to her, I stood in the dark with her—waiting for my name to be called into the microphone, waiting to march up the stairs, and onto center stage.

Taking a deep breath, I pressed away all the anxiety. Not allowing the fear to take over, I quietly disarmed the panic threatening to destroy my future. I double-checked my simple ponytail and did a 'once-over' across my plain and dark coloured attire.

The choice was key.

Nothing too bright, nothing too flashy, there was to be nothing for them to ogle over that would draw the crowd out of the message. This is about them, helping them. And maybe just a bit about me. I nodded my head to no one, silently going over my inner pep talk.

"I am not afraid, I am excited. I am awesome, I am powerful, I am going to change and empower not only my life but the lives of others." I whispered to myself, flexing my fingers and shaking them out.

And then, as the timekeeper announced my name, the mental switch of whom I was to whom I was meant to be, flicked on. The bright overhead lights turned, following my practiced and precise stride out onto the stage then shone down on the powerful woman who I built by my need of existence.

The one who, by opening her mouth and letting her soul sing out, took the crowd by storm.

Chapter 5

The loud roar of applause woke me from my dream like state. A flood of exhilarated energy danced through my soul and I bowed to the unexpected standing ovation these beautiful souls gave to me in a show of appreciation for what my few heartfelt words had given them. I was so high right now that I could have easily flown down to my seat without once touching the floor.

As the timekeeper approached me with clapping hands and a hopeful gleam in his eyes, I sweetly grinned at him and nodded. I waved to the still standing crowd then turned back towards the darkness of the curtains and took a step. My legs nearly gave out and I stumbled just a bit.

Gritting my teeth, I willed myself to move forward.

"Now is not the time for your silly awkwardness to ruin everything, Andy...get moving," My inner voice yelled at me in a strangely calm but irritated tone.

I turned once more to the crowd and smiled, seeing a few of them gasp at my small stumble but waved once more as my feet finally decided to play nice and not make me look like a drunken idiot.

With a loud exhale, I set myself down into my assigned chair, shaking a bit from the exhaustion of adrenalin that kept me running on full steam on stage. Tucking myself neatly back into the fold of presenters, now all glued to my every move, I tried to still my thrumming pulse. So many beaming faces, smiles of mere politeness before, had cultivated real genuine reflections of respect and awe. I knew I wasn't much to look at, but I was astonished by the fact that my simple choice of dress and hairstyle had been that effective in making me nearly invisible before, and my inner skills almost non-existent. My mind wandered away from the excited rumblings of the aftershock of my performance, debating the pros and cons of my stealthy disguise.

A shuffling noise on the floor drew my dazed eyes to a couple of my sheets that had escaped their folder.

Bending down under the table to retrieve them, the timekeeper announced that this speaker would be the last presentation of the day. The low hum of excited voices murmured across the room and under the table—some eager to leave and seek out the city's tourist attractions—while others excited for the night's social hour. I reached for the last of my papers and prayed for the poor sap that managed to get this time slot. I thought mine was a tough gig, but the last one of the day was a killer.

You had to be a rock star in order to find the attention span of anyone, even me. And I liked this crap.

A smoky rough voice sang into the mic, thanking the speaker then proceeded to address the crowd. Low hushed twitters of strangely bizarre mumblings took over the noise under the table.

That's odd, I thought, wondering what in the world has got everyone in such a state.

"I would like to thank you all for staying tuned in this long. I know it's been a long day and you are all no doubt eager to get out of here and begin socializing. To tell you the truth so am I. So, I beg of you all to bear with me just a little bit longer. But I'm not sure how anyone would be able to shine now...especially after that life-changing demonstration we just had from Miss Andy Morrison."

My head jolted upwards at the loud sultry sound of my name being spoken, cracking the back of my head on the underside of the table.

"Let's have another round of applause for her ability to blow the roof off of this convention. Where is she?"

Panic hit me. All my collected papers escape from my hands, dropping back to the floor. I scurried to grab them back up and pull myself free from my confinements, rubbing at the soreness throbbing at the top of my ponytail—hands clutching onto the crumpled pile of notes.

Turning towards the crowd and waving once again, I pasted a wide smile on my crimson stained face, seeing the hope in their eyes burrowing deeper into their subconscious. Then turn to give thanks to the speaker. "Oh, sweet mother of..." is all my mind could conjure up. My jaw nearly dropped, unhinged by what I found staring down at me from above on the stage. But with a swift clench of my teeth, it stayed shut—held by a strangely awkward smile.

Where the hell did this guy come from? I wondered, my body tingling from just making eye contact with him. In my recent travels from my newly discovered journey of life, I have seen a few striking men but holy sweet mother of Pearl, this was something right out of a wet dream. He wasn't pretty but downright beautiful—gifted with a rawness to his looks and obviously was possessed with the magical ability to make smart girls forget how to talk.

My mouth dried up and my throat closed in—the capability to even form a logical word to reply to him...poof, gone.

So I just waved and nodded my head. No need in showing him the inner bumbling geek that I was so desperately trying to contain.

He smiled and nodded as if he understood something I had not—the heat in my face nearly cooking me alive in the brief few second of exchange. I promptly lowered myself down, reaching out with my free hand and seeking out the back of my chair so I wouldn't go ass over tea kettle onto the floor—my outstanding lecture notes still grasped tightly against my chest, crumpled.

"As you all have guessed by now, I am not *the* Warren Matthews that was supposed to be standing here tonight but I assure you I am indeed Warren Matthews...just junior." He smirked, his mouth curling up on one side of his full lips—ice blue in his eyes dancing like water through moonlight and that body...his motions were rhythmic and precise, like a cat stalking prey. It was hypnotic to watch and I leaned in on my hand just to try to focus better on what he had to say. "But to the rest of the world, I am better known as Shayne Matthews. And I will be your speaker tonight in place of my father."

The crowd applauded, some giggled and sniggered—rightly so, he didn't even have to talk, just existing on stage was enough to wake anyone up and take notice. "I hope I can do my father proud and attempt to fill his shoes on stage. But I think it's going to be tough to even come close to what Miss Morrison has contributed to our reason for gathering here this weekend."

He twisted his attentions directly on me. My pulse raced as a crooked grin grew over his lips and he winked at me before turning back to the crowd once more. My hands lost feeling and my papers found the floor again as my mind reeled. "Did he just wink at me?"

Chapter 6

Over the next forty-five minutes, my eyes stayed glued on the tall figure, marching with ease across the stage merely a few feet in front of me. His eyes focused on the crowd. His words, strong but kind as he spoke to the people about having pride in what they do, about being accountable for what they created and contributed to the lively hood of the companies they work for.

To tell you the truth, after a while, I wasn't entirely sure what the hell he was saying up there. I was a slave to just watching, and absorbing the movements of his body as he masterfully strode in front of the masses all erect yet at ease. Obviously, someone who has become one with who they were and able to manifest his presence to perfection, that pulled you in and kept you eager to be there—on the edge of your seat, hoping he would get close enough for you to touch or to smell the subtle scent of his essence.

My head was drawn and rested on the palm of my hand as I dreamily stared. Imagining what he looked like underneath that pale blue cotton dress shirt and those pleated grey dress pants that hung loosely in all the right places.

My body responded to every damn move this man made. A slowly heated ache began to build in places that conferences were not supposed to invoke.

This was complete and utter madness, nearing on torture. Especially, when he made it a point to stride to the left side of the stage, and hover just above the table where I was desperately trying to stay upright in my chair. Not to mention, trying to keep both hands visible and on the table while one begged to be let loose and find the furious spot between my legs.

This was so unprofessional of me.

Never once, in my two years of building this career of speaking, did anyone—not even my own 'boyfriend', caused this kind of reaction from just being in the same space together.

Madness, I say.

But I'll take it. Hard against a wall, his hands stroking me from beneath while he...

Whoa, I exhaled with a shake of my head, rattling myself back to earth. My mind abruptly cleared with the thunder of applause taking over the room. Shayne Matthews' time on stage ended just like that. With a quick thank you for being here and a well wish to the crowd, hoping they enjoyed the non-working weekend ahead of them, he was gone into the darkness of the curtains.

A soft low voice from my right interrupted my search for his ghost in the crowd. "Wasn't he marvellous?"

I turned, still caught in the strange spell he had cast on me, and from the dreamy look the older lady had smeared all over her face he had apparently cast it on her as well.

How could he not?

He was tall and broad like a Viking. His face, strong and defined. He wore a no-nonsense kind of manner about him that immediately screamed at you, and your libido apparently, demanding your fullest attention. It was only the soft curl of his dirty blond hair that took away from his edged look. A more playful side to his features that made you let your guard down while he snuck in and robbed your senses of their logical side.

"Oh yes," I concurred. He was a marvellous creature.

"I really took away some hot tips that will help me get my company moving in the right direction. What parts did you like?"

Not wanting to let on that my brain had totally been hijacked by an unnatural animalistic desire to lure him away into a dark corner and rip his clothes off, not to mention bite him hard everywhere, then ride him into next week. No, that would probably be highly unproductive for my future.

But I had heard nothing.

Any helpful words from this smoking hot god, who just poured out his soul for almost an hour, were lost on me. He, no doubt, donated a mountain of business knowledge that I probably should have been taking notes on.

But did I? Nope. Not a one.

With a quick exhale, letting go of my lost opportunity, I poured a bucket of cold water on my suddenly unruly libido which denied me any of this and answered her, "All of it."

What else was I supposed to say without looking like a fraud in front of my peers? Too busy ogling over a boy like a lovesick teenager. This was not going to win me any votes of confidence.

"Oh, I quite agree. He is a business genius just like his father."

I smiled, my face flushing a bit, wishing the old geezer had actually attended the conference like I had expected him to do. Warren S. Matthews senior was actually one of the other speakers I wanted to check off my bucket list this weekend but I guess I was going to have keep him on the list just a little longer.

Damn him and his ridiculous, hectic business schedule. How dare he send his son to speak in his place? Damn him straight to... my mind drifted off once again remembering the way the not quite Scottish drawl curled about his lips as W.S. Matthews junior spoke. I could feel the change in my body temperature as it rose just thinking about him.

Damn it.

"Are you catching a bite at the hotel before the meet and greet at eight?"

Her words pulled me back in and wiped away Mister I am too smart to be this sexy from my mind. "Oh, um, actually I was thinking of taking a quick stroll, seeing a bit of the city first before the gathering. I found a brochure on my night table with a couple of restaurants that seemed nearby."

"I don't blame you, dear, the food here is wonderful. I think all I did was eat the last time I visited Saint John's," she said tapping her finger against her lip, trying to remember something, "What was that place again? Hmm, oh yes, now I remember. It's called Chester's or something like that. It's not fancy, mind you, but if you like fish and chips you just have to go there before you head back home."

"I love fish n' chips," I said smiling at her, "I'll to try to remember that."

"You do that," she said gathering up her things and walking toward the exit like everyone else, "See you later."

With a wave of her hand, she was gone.

I leaned back against the wall of the elevator, listening to my stomach give me the *what not* about depriving it of any nourishment since noon, and wondering where I had placed those pamphlets. I only had about an hour and a half before eight, surely there would be something close enough for me to sneak in and grab a bite.

Quickly dropping my papers onto the bed, I pulled on my black ultralight hip flared blazer and headed back down to the lobby, ready to start exploring—only stopping for a minute to check in with the front desk for any messages I may have missed.

Nope, radio silence. Nothing.

My heart sank, I had half hoped Jeremy would have at least called me or surprised me with a bouquet of flowers or something—anything at all. After all, it was my birthday tomorrow.

But nothing...yet.

I'm not sure why I kept setting myself up to be disappointed every year, every holiday, hoping he would just do something that was wild and crazy and unexpected...or anything that showed me I was at least on his radar.

But he never did.

Right then and there, the decision maker that lurked down deep inside of me—the one that came to surface whenever it was my time to speak, the one I was hurriedly building up with this new life I was making—made a decision...one I had been struggling with for way too long about my relationship with Jeremy.

Staying with someone just because they were there, most of the time...who am I kidding? Once in a while, and willing to somewhat willing to participate as a couple, was no reason to stay there.

We didn't live together. We never spent holidays together. He only stayed at my place every other weekend, and we didn't even live in the same city.

He did always make it a point to call every night, regardless of what was going on, but it was wearing thin on my emotional connection with him. Even though it was nice having someone to talk to about things, whenever he made time to listen, I could feel something changing.

And I am not sure if it was even his fault.

His life kept him in his city. I could, I guess, move to where he was but it had never come up, not really. Only once, did we ever discuss anything close to doing that but was quickly shot down by a phone call he just *had* to take.

Why was I slowly killing myself over someone that obviously had no desire to 'change'...anything?

Somewhere lost in my meanderings, I had actually wandered too far, missing the street I was supposed to take and was way off course. I laughed aloud, allowing the new and decisive part of me take over.

"On this weekend away, on your birthday weekend no less, if he does not make some kind of small effort, then it was time to cut him loose and move on," I said out loud, making a deal with myself.

Because did I really want to go on being someone's sometime girlfriend? Hell, I had only met his mother once and that was over a year ago.

Turning myself around and pulling my phone out of my pocket, I looked at the time and sighed. My appetite lost, just as much as I was.

A loud crack of thunder sounded across the sky. Wind picked up, swirling my hair, and whipped me in the face with the end of my ponytail. The scent of fresh water washed through the air before the sky above opened up and unleashed its fury on me.

"Oh, come on!" I growled, pulling the edge of my coat up around my ears, turning on my heels and hurrying back in the direction that I came, trying to retrace my steps. Caught within the torrential downpour now cleansing the city with its sweet smell from the ocean's salty fragrance, I stop and begrudgingly pulled out my phone barely able to see two feet in front of me—looking for the GPS app I had installed.

Standing alone in the middle of Saint Johns, lost, and unable to get the friggen' app to work long enough to punch in my coordinates, I heard a somewhat familiar sultry voice call out my name through the thundering rain.

Slowly turning, I placed my arm over the top of my eyes, shielding them from the downpour.

Crap!

"Miss Morrison, do you need a lift?"

His ice blue eye shone through lowered window, shadows playing on his tanned skin making them seem even bluer than they probably were. My stomach flipped, butterflies swarmed within, strangling me from my ability to speak. All I could do was nod before rushing down off the sidewalk and towards his car. Pulling the door wide, I jumped in, and closed out the storm—unknowingly surrounded myself within another.

Chapter 7

Oh, my...sweet merciful... I was barely able to breathe. *How can someone look like that?*

The subtle smells of exotic essential oils mixed with the soft musk of his skin lingering in the air reminded me of my patchouli candle I burned every time I read at home. I swore just looking into his eyes made my thighs tighten.

My panties suddenly felt damp.

Get a hold of yourself, Andy, My inner logical voice cursed, pulling on my animalistic side as it kicked and screamed to be let loose. I bit my bottom lip, hard, trying to get a grip on my senses and turned away.

"Heading back to the hotel for the meet and greet?" Shayne Mathews hummed so sultry and low it vibrated across my soul.

I nodded. My hair, completely drenched from the rain, fell into my face and stuck there—poking me in the eye. "Yes," I finally muttered out, trying to make my mouth, and my brain, work, "You?"

He blew out a slow breath. The smell of fresh mint drifted into the mix of smells. My tongue ran over my lip, wondering if his mouth would taste the same.

"I don't normally do these kinds of events but my father was called away on business. I'm here out of obligation to the company—a face for everyone to place in front of a worthy cause."

"Oh," I coughed out. *Of course he's not going to the meet and greet. He fulfilled his responsibility to his company with us. His time is way too important to mingle with the peasants.* The words rolled loudly around in my head as I stared out into the night through the flapping wipers.

"So do you believe in what this convention represents? That it is needed within the workplace?"

There she goes! I cheered, brain re-engaged. Libido...still engaged but overruled.

"No, not at first, I thought this to be nothing more than a waste of time," he admitted, watching the lights of the hotel slowly come into view, making the ice in his eyes flare in the darkness. He flicked his blinker on, "But today, I heard something that validated my father's decision to put his brand on it this event, and sponsor it, as well as hold it in our hotel."

"Oh..." I dared to look at him one more time as we pulled up to the front doors. "Do you mind if I ask what those words were?"

The bright lights lit up the space like the fourth of July as he placed the car into park.

I waited for his answer.

His grin was so sweet I couldn't help biting my bottom lip and thinking things I shouldn't be thinking about him. My panties definitely soaking as whispers, in a low sweet Scottish burr, drawled out of him, "I suggest you check your notes Miss Morrison...the parts about only being granted one life, and the power to make a difference. You've a clever mind. I'm sure you'll have no trouble finding it."

My breath caught as his mouth curled back into his impish grin, lips twisted into the most kiss-worthy pose. I glanced over at the size of his fingers. The kaleidoscope of wild butterflies took flight again within my stomach, flying much lower, tickling against my more sensitive parts now aching to be touched— begging for attention from the hands that fell loosely over his leather steering wheel.

I swallowed hard gathering my senses, and my ability to speak, glad my pants were soaked from rain because they sure as hell were wet now.

"Thank you again, for stopping and saving me from drowning in the streets."

"It was my pleasure, Miss Morrison, have a wonderful evening."

"Goodnight, Mr. Matthews."

The rain poured down into the doorman's face as he promptly pulled the door open for me and I stepped out, feeling bad that he had to face the bad weather. But his warm smile never faltered as he wished me a good evening.

Catching one more glimpse of Shayne Matthews over my shoulder, I walked towards the revolving doors and inhaled a deep breath, trying to recover from being drunk on his beauty. Peculiar looks, given to me as I entered the lobby from gathering folks heading to the meet and greet social, made me wondered if it was because I had just stepped out of Mr. Morrison's car. But soon, after catching my reflection in the glass doors, I clued in and shuddered.

My face, plastered with straggled locks of wet hair, wore rings of black paint that bordered somewhere between Gothic and raccoonish.

Well, isn't that just perfect?

It's not like I'd ever see the man again, but this is what he would recall whenever the name Andy Morrison ever came up again.

Yup...just perfect.

Hurrying into the lobby, I came to the definite conclusion that I really needed a drink.

Chapter 8

The hotel lobby was filled with the loud buzz of excited bodies making their way back in through the hall, some of it from the bar I had visited earlier this morning and some coming from further down the hall in the conference room. I promptly made my way to the front desk and waited for the receptionist to finish checking in the elderly couple just ahead of me. My eyes followed the sounds of merriment once more, mixed with a musical undertone that made me smile despite my embarrassing look. I couldn't remember the last time I went out where there was music.

A cheery voice drew my attention, just as the elderly couple stepped away blocking my view of the hall. "Good evening Miss, can I help you with anything?"

"Ah, yes, hi. I was just wondering if there were any messages for me. I just stepped out for a bit."

Her grin grew a bit larger, her eyes twinkling in the light. "Looks like the storm found you."

My hands reached for my hair tucking the loose strand of wet hair behind my ear. "That it did. The weather changes fast here."

"That it does," she giggles, "Can I have your name?"

"Miss Morrison."

Her eyes widened, and a small gasp left her. "Oh, Miss Morrison, I'm sorry I didn't recognize you. I loved your presentation earlier, I was lucky enough to catch it before my shift started. Everything you said in there was brilliant, and it felt as if every word was meant for me." Her face lit up, giddiness in her body language sung through her as she continued to go on about how she was going to try to follow all the important points she had taken note of.

This...this is what it was all about.

Even if I had only reached one person, gave one person a new perspective of how important it was to take control of their lives and make it their own. This made all my hard work worth it.

"That is wonderful to hear. I'm so glad you enjoyed it," I encouraged, and let her go on a bit until she finished. "Are there any messages?"

"Oh sorry," she said peeking over my shoulder seeing there had become a bit of a line up while she expressed her enthusiasm about her new life path. "I prattled your ears nearly off. What room again?"

"No worries, it's the Marilyn Suite."

A flick of her brow and a quick grin, she turned and peeked into the box marked with a gold plate stamped with a large black 'M'.

"Sorry," she said returning to the desk, "No messages."

My heart sank a bit but I smiled anyway, thanking her. Then hurried across the lobby floor toward the elevator and pressed the up button. A loud ding slid the doors open and I stepped inside, greeted by a horrific sight.

"Oh, my...crap."

No wonder everyone was looking at me weird. Quickly stepping into the elevator, I edged closer to the mirror pressing my thumb under my eye, rubbing away the black smear. Horror struck me and I felt like a fool. Not the confident and brilliant woman who had stood on stage spouting earth-shattering advice but as a pathetic drowned creature, that Shayne Matthews rescued like a stray off the streets.

I exhaled and dropped my hands, turning my back to the beast and leaned against the mirror. I didn't know why this bothered me so much. But it did.

It bothered me fiercely.

The chime of the elevator brought me back, welcoming me to the top floor. Marching toward my room, I decided I was being pathetic.

All this energy I was wasting on worrying was exactly the kind of thing I preached to others. Maybe it was time I took my own advice. I couldn't change what I had looked like and what's done was done. It was superficial and shallow.

Would this affect my future? Probably not.

So I let it go. No longer wasting anymore of my precious time on it.

After a quick shower to warm up and a change of clothes, I raided the black fridge. Stuffing a complimentary wedge of cheese into my mouth, I marched back out into the hall. Sucking up my embarrassment, I hit the down button and headed for the lobby.

Chapter 9

The sweet bite of ginger mixed with the soft burn of rye on my tongue was just what the doctor ordered. The room buzzed with so much life, and the energy of all the warm bodies that filled it was intoxicating.

Long forgotten was the bedraggled image of the drenched raccoon, and here to represent was Andy Morrison, future leader, and inspirational guru.

It was easy to feel good around these people, especially since the hard part was over. No longer was I part of the show, I was here to take in the rest of the conference as a spectator and a student of knowledge as well.

My smile was genuine as I watched everyone mingle and engage in conversation. I even began to enjoy the few people who were brave enough to approach me and strike up a conversation. Once the drinks kicked in and the lights were dimmed, I even made my way to the dance floor now constructed in the middle of the room.

This was what it was all about.

The interaction with people, with my peers, making connections and enjoying being in the moment of life, this was what I was here for. No more drooling over gorgeous impromptu speakers—only here as a last minute change.

Everything would be back to the strict schedule I had planned out.

Taking a break from the gathering of women who had dragged me out onto the floor, I wandered back into the crowd and moseyed up to the bar for another Ginger and Rye. Leaned back onto the edge of the bar, I watched the incredible show of life as it happened all around me.

"You look like you are enjoying yourself," the low sultry voice cut through the music, tickling the edge of my ear. I turned to answer it, a heartfelt smile of appreciation drawn across my face.

"Yes, it has been a fun event so fa..." My voice caught in my throat, realizing to whom the comment belonged to.

Eyes the colour of a summer sky greeted me, cloaked within shadows and dimmed light, and set upon a face so breathtakingly handsome that it stole my breath. A wave of embarrassment burned on my cheeks remembering exactly how I had looked the last time we spoke. All the confidence I brought with me here into this place, all of it that I gained here on the stage, dwindled to mere vapours.

What the hell was wrong with me?

I didn't even know this man and he somehow had managed to destroy every ounce of my strength with just a few words. What was he holding in his pocket, kryptonite? And for that matter, what in the hell was he doing here anyway—ruining my simple weekend of learning and…what the hell?

Determined to fight this strange power he had cast over me, I pushed back the poor pathetic hormone induced teenager whirling inside and took a sip of my drink—bringing forth the woman determined to stay in control of my world.

"Are you lost?"

The creases deepened at the corner of his eyes as his mouth curled crookedly on the left then turning to the bartender he ordered a drink. "I'm not sure."

"I thought you said these events weren't your kind of *thing*."

"They're not," he hummed merrily.

"Then why are you here?" My voice, just a little too sharp as I quizzed him about being present at his own function. *Too bold maybe*, I thought but whatever. He was supposed to be long gone and letting me get on with my weekend. Not here, in my face, way too close and looking way too bloody hot.

"Let's just say I had a change of heart."

His words were so daring. His eyes even more so as he locked his gaze on me, stepping into my space smelling like a midnight summers' dream.

A rush of heat swept over me. Tingling stirred again in places that had just been cooled. What in the hell was going on with me? Even the centers of my palms were starting to sweat.

Gripping my fingers tighter around the short glass of rye, I took another sip then pulled it close to my body—hopefully ensuring I didn't drop it on myself by mistake.

"You seem to be a natural people magnet."

I peeked over my shoulder just enough to steal a quick glimpse at him as his body turned into mine so close I could feel the heat of his torso against my bared arm. He was too close—dangerously too close, my body begged to lean into his warmth. "And how exactly would you know this?"

"Because I have been watching you all night."

He what? "You what?"

"It's not very often that my curiosity of someone is intrigued."

"No?"

"No."

"And why is that?" I swallowed hard.

"Because people are predictable and boring—the ones that aren't are dangerous."

"Are you calling me boring?"

A low chuckle escaped him and he turned to face the masses of convention goers enjoying themselves, letting go of their inhibitions as the music played on and the drinks flowed freely.

"No, quite the opposite."

"Oh, so now I'm dangerous?"

He huffed out a breathy laugh. "Maybe, but I find the way you see the world to be quite...refreshing."

"Oh, well that is a relief. I would hate for you to feel as if your presenters didn't live up to their standards of preached philosophies."

"I have no doubt Miss Morrison, that your world spins through this life on an axle you have deliberately set."

Okay, so maybe I should cut him some slack—at least he was trying to seem insightful. "Okay, so tell me something, Mr. Matthews. Since this is not exactly your 'thing', what is it that makes your world spin?"

Setting his empty glass onto the bar he slowly leaned into me, eyes narrowed and darkened, then whispered into my ear, "You really want to know?"

His breath was hot against my skin, lips nearly grazing mine as he slowly pulled away. I inhaled, catching his scent—so subtle and alluring in his closeness that I felt dizzy. I had no idea who this man was but my entire being just seemed to be drawn to him not to mention everything about him set my body into a fiery rage.

"Yes." My answer slid slowly across my lips. It was all I could make myself say as butterflies in my belly fluttered below.

"Then finish your drink and I'll show you."

Oh, gaud, was he serious? He can't be serious.

I am not the kind of girl that acts this way.

I don't run off into the night, in a strange city, with a stranger no less. This was totally not a good idea, highly illogical, and irresponsible but right now all I wanted to do rush forward, to see what he was about and what his mouth tasted like—to find out if it was sweet or minty, the way it smelled of mint and ginger. It was all I could do to stay still, and to not press my mouth against his.

Not able to see clearly anymore—the blue of his eyes so intensely focused just on me, I stayed quiet for a minute—trying to debate my answer.

"That is unless you have other plans tonight."

My eyes glanced down at his wrist, studying the face on his watch. Almost ten thirty.

Tell him you do. Tell him you have to get up early in the morning. Say anything. You can't just run off with him into the night. That's not who you are.

"No," I choked out.

"No you don't want to see or no you don't have any other plans?"

"No, I don't have any other plans."

"Good." Is all he said, "Shall we then?"

I shook my head and swallowed down the last of my drink, slowly placing the empty glass on the bar and looked up at him, not sure if this was really happening.

He draped an arm around my back not actually touching me but the heat of his closeness guiding me toward the exit. My legs shook, my heart pounded as I went willingly out of the safety net of my hotel and into the night.

Chapter 10

Staring out into the night, peeking through the window, I watched as the city passed by us in smears of light while he drove through it in his black Beemer. Stopping no more than three or four streets away from the hotel, he pulled the car up into a dark alleyway and put it into park.

Oh, crap...what have I done? He might be drop-dead gorgeous, but so was Ted Bundy, and we all know how that turned out. I reached for the door debating whether or not to jump out and run just as he opened his own door, blinding me with the overhead light in the car.

He loosened a soft chuckle. "Don't worry I didn't bring you into this dark alley to murder you."

My face heated, no doubt he had read the expression of my inner dialogue easily. "It's just the backway into the building. It can get a little crazy here on the weekends, so we're taking a shortcut in."

The door closed, leaving me in the darkness—trying to compose myself. My nerves of being out like this obviously were getting the best of me. I willingly said yes to this adventure, so I guess it was time to put on my big girl panties and see what happens. Reaching for the handle but the door opened before I could pull it. Shayne stood behind holding it open in the rain.

"Are you still sure you want to know, Miss Morrison? I can take you back to the hotel if you like."

Here was my opening to head back to the safety zone.

I swung my legs out onto the pavement and let him close the door behind me. Grabbing my hand, he hauled me around the front of the car and under the small covering over the door. The low thud of a bass boomed quick muffled beats from behind the big black door in front of us as Shayne pulled out his keys and wiggled them into the lock.

"You own a night club?"

He continued to wiggle the lock, only glancing at me for a second. "Yes, among other things."

I never saw him as the club owner kind of type. Too well-kept, too controlled. But I guess these would be great qualities to have in whatever line of business he chose. The Matthews family was a Multi-million dollar corporation with their Hotel chains I supposed a night club wouldn't be that far off the mark. Business was business as long as they were a lucrative investment.

With a loud click the lock freed, and he turned to me flicking his brow. "You ready?"

"Ready as I'll ever be," I said, raising my brow—a nervous giggle escaping me.

Not sure how this would turn out, spending the evening at a night club. I was never one who spent much time in them, except for when my best friend Kimmie used to drag me there now and then, especially the first year we turned of age to drink. It was a right-of-passage she said, insisting I joined her whenever she went and once again before I left for the city. We drifted away from each other since but it's just the way life goes sometimes.

What would she say if she could see me now?

Out and about, completely out of my comfort zone. With a man I didn't know and that was totally out of my league.

Yeah, she would be shocked but...wicked proud, no doubt.

Pulling the door wide, he yelled out over the blast of music, "Let's go."

I shook my head just as he took my hand and hauled me through the back door, letting it close on the world outside and cloaking me in darkness. His body brushed up against mine, warm and electric. His hand stayed tight around mine as loud thrashing music deafened me immediately but I continued, stumbling behind him, being pulled through the dark.

Giddiness swirled through me and I started to laugh. This had to be the most bizarre night of my life. "Watch the stairs," he yelled out just a couple seconds too late. I nearly wiped out, my foot fetching up on the bottom of the steps he had just warned me about.

"Are you alright, Morrison?" he said, stopping to help me back up.

"Just peachy," I hollered, still half giggling and trying to keep up with him as we marched up the stairs, "Where exactly are you dragging me to?"

As the words fell out of my mouth, the edge of darkness bloomed all around us in an array of shooting colours.

"To an Atomic Paradise," he announced, stepping out from behind a fake wall and onto a balcony. We stood speechless, overlooking a sea of moving bodies, dancing provocatively to the rhythm of the night.

I stilled watching them—observing them from a safe distance, having fun and living freely if only for these few moments. It wasn't as overwhelming as I'd remembered from my own adventures of youth. A smile curled on my lips then turned to Shayne, feeling his eyes on me again. His eyes sparkled, that crooked smile drawing me under again into his magical spell.

He was like a quiet storm brewing in front of me.

One that I wanted to get lost in and to dance within his strange gentle rain.

Chapter 11

We crowd-watched, lost in their movements for a few moments before he asked me what I would like to drink—leaving me to stand on my own while he went to fetch us a couple of drinks from the bar below.

I leaned over the edge of the railing, watching him slice through the crowd, melting seamlessly into them—smiling and waving until he reached the edge of the bar.

He was so much taller from up here compared to most of everyone else. His blue dress shirt stood out like a beacon against the darker clothing others wore. My eyes stayed glued to him, watching while he unbuttoned his sleeves and rolled them up just below the bend of his elbow—revealing strong, defined forearms, which moved and shadowed, as he gripped the edge of the bar. It was hard not to swoon over him from up here. A smile settled permanently on my lips, watching him interacted so smoothly and gracefully.

As if he could hear my thoughts his eyes lifted and bore into mine, something hungry in his gaze made me bite the edge of my lip—a low moan escaping my throat, swallowed up by the sound of the bar around me.

In all my life, I have never felt this alive, this awake, and...this confused all at the same time over being near a man.

Even when I met Jeremy, it was never what I would call electric.

He was cute. He thought I was cute. He asked me out so I said yes.

No fireworks, no butterflies causing havoc in my stomach. Well, maybe a few but nothing compared to the wild ones that took flight every time I got anywhere near Shayne.

This was something different—something unexpected and...it was nice.

And there was no need to feel guilty in any way.

It's not like I was out on a date or anything. I was just two professional speakers hanging out—one of which offered some local hospitality, to show me some of the sights, and to have a drink.

Besides, Jeremy was probably out doing god knows what wherever he was.

He hadn't stayed over in weeks—something to do with trying to catch up on his workload, or so he said. And I knew I was guilty of letting work consume me too but this whole long distant, infrequent relationship was wearing thin on me just the same.

"They only had Copper Rye, I hope you don't mind."

His words made me jump. I was buried so far into my excuses to not feel guilty I didn't notice him leaving the bar or sneaking up on me.

"You alright? You look a little lost."

With a quick inhale, catching a light whiff of Shayne's intoxicating scent, I shook my head no. "Sorry just going over the presentation I did earlier. Trying to find ways to tweak it...make it better."

"Well from where I was standing, I thought it was perfect, and there's no need in fixing something that isn't broken," he said, handing me my drink, "I saw the way the people looked at you. I saw faces transform hearing the truth spoken in your words. It was pretty damn spot on if you ask me, you should be proud."

My mouth curled up, watching him light up the darkness as he spoke, and wondered about which precise words were the reason that drug him out of his cave—to want to bring me here with him.

Gaud he was so damn beautiful.

I shook my head, trying to compose myself and to form a coherent sentence. "So this is what makes you tick?"

"Nah, this is only part of it...the real action is back there."

He pointed back towards the fake wall we had entered through earlier. I flicked a brow at him this time, wondering what in the hell was behind door number three.

"Don't be looking at me like that. Do you want to see or not?"

"I'm here aren't I?"

He laughed and gave his head a shake. "That you are Miss Morrison," he said, pulling out his keys again, he turned away and headed back into the darkness once more.

Chapter 12

The overhead lights flickered on, casting a soft glow over the room. Leatherback chairs set to each side of a large wooden desk. Piles of paperwork neatly stacked on each side of it with colourful sticky tabs protruding out of the edges of each one. A red velvet pool table with antique wooden carved legs stood in the center of the space while a small library decorated the back wall from floor to ceiling, filled with words that looked old and new.

Along the edges of the room, a half-wall ran along the sides. Soft grey worn wood wrapped around the bottom, while the top of it was lined with a collection of framed awards and certificates, all business accomplishments, from what I could tell.

I followed him into the light, sipping my drink but left him to inspect the wall of frames more closely.

A Master's degree in this, highest achievement award for that, the walls literally screamed out his brilliance in business know-how. No wonder his father felt it a safe choice to leave him behind to represent his Hotel and business dynasty. He was definitely qualified to preach about putting forth the effort or whatever the hell he said up there—still feeling a bit agitated by losing all that time daydreaming about him, obviously his speech had been brilliant by how the crowd had continued to chatter on about it afterwards at the meet and greet.

I exhaled, giving myself a silent scolding and moved on. Sipping my drink I decided, given the opportunity, I would make a mend for my moment of...well, body-lust—I guessed would be a good name for it, and put this up-close and personal opportunity, I had so strangely found myself in now, to good use.

"So you like learning I see," I teased, peaking at him over my shoulder.

He gave a quick laugh, shrugging his shoulders. His eyes grazed over me while his hands busied themselves, digging for something in one of his desk drawers.

With a slow rise of his left brow, a devilish intense gaze burned in his eyes. The wall of books dislodged from its resolute position behind him, and slid forward, then broke apart in two directions— revealing French doors behind, glass panes painted by frost against the dark mahogany coloured rich wood that held them in place.

"What are you some kind of James Bond?"

"I don't think the legendary spy would take kindly to having being compared to someone like me," he hummed sliding the doors wide and into the walls.

I edged around the desk, cautiously following him and his cheeky grin, wondering who on earth this man was.

His large well-toned frame entered into the shadows of the opened doors, disappearing from sight. Soft rows of light lit up the space in front of him as he moved forward. Soft yellow lighting set his hair to shine in shades of sand and shadows—raw masculine features of his face became refined and smoothened. And the way his body moved so precise, so measured and sure, struck a strange tingling across my flesh—warming everything from the inside out—an animalistic lure of a dominant mate now on display, sang to all the right parts of the female quietly watching, assessing if he would be a good partner for coupling.

My body began to ache just watching him move, it had decidedly proclaimed without a doubt he passed any and every test in the game and would not be kicked out of bed for any reason.

My breast firmed against my shirt, stretching the cotton tight, nipples wide-awake and pressed to their fullest attention—obviously traitors to my attempted façade of being in control. I wrapped my arms around me and held my drink close to my chest in efforts to hide what this man was doing to me and how wildly erotic it felt to follow him into the unknown.

And, I did it willingly—excited to see just how deep this rabbit hole went.

Shapes manifested as the lights sprang to life around us. To the right, a corner couch hugged part of the back wall, rounded to hover in front of a fireplace now bursting to life and glowing in red and gold embers—set within another wall of books, shelves upon shelves of words lined the entire space.

Continuing on to follow my host, who now stood beside a long narrow slab of marble, lined with three black cushioned seats and lit by long slender tubes, which hung down from the ceiling—lights merged together into one continual glow across the speckled surface.

Haunting in the background were chrome tinted appliances, a fridge, stove and sink all pressed neatly in amongst dark rich chocolate coloured cupboards that climbed to the ceiling.

Shayne's mouth curled crookedly, lines pinching the edge of his eyes as he watched me over his shoulder taking it all in.

"You live here," I said, sipping down the last of my drink, "over the bar?"

"Most of the time," he retorted, sliding in around the marble slab. "I like being near people and their sounds of living without actually having to be with them."

Odd, I thought to myself but I kind of got it. I might not live over a loud thrumming night club filled to the brim with bodies and loud music but I did choose an apartment that was downtown nestled in amongst the heart of the city—often leaving my windows open in the summer months just to hear the heartbeat of the world outside.

Maybe not so odd after all, I hummed retracting my previous thought.

Edging towards the bar, I set my drink on the cold surface. His large nimble fingers reached for my glass. "Can I freshen up your drink?"

I pulled the glass back, suddenly aware that maybe I should have some water instead. A low grumble from my stomach reminded me I had indeed failed at feeding it properly over the last few hours. The cheese I had taken out of the mini fridge had been used up and digested long ago. Another drink would surely put me over the limit of cognizance and straight into non-sensible things. An absolute fact I found out from my few attempts at drinking with Kimmie every now and again.

"Actually, a drink of water would be great."

He stepped away from the bar and slid in front of me, a hand slipped forward, fingers grazing over mine as he pulled the glass free from my hand.

My face heated, rushed with emotion from his closeness—washing over me, hurting me gently in all the places that could get me into trouble if I listened to their begging need to just touch him.

I blinked my eyes hard to get rid of the vision of him my mind had just conjured up—dangerously curious about the subtle curves that touched perfectly against his cotton shirt, and charcoal grey pants. Watching him walk toward his fridge was driving my libido into overdrive—that glass of water was indeed a better choice than the rye.

"I only have a couple of bottles of carbonated water, will that do? I would offer you some tap water but it might be more potent than the rye you were drinking." Shayne's laughter sang out of him in a sound that was so light, so lyrical that I couldn't help but smile.

I found him so curiously strange and beautiful— his subtle moves slowly making me crazy.

That's it...I was going crazy.

That has got to be it—it just has to be. This whole situation of me running off into the night with him and now in his hideaway home was totally insane. And yet I stayed.

"That's perfect, thank you."

Grabbing two bottles of the water in one hand and a large platter in the other he started back, passing in front of me with a flick of his brow. "You coming?"

My mind, whirling with ridiculous pheromones, said not yet but was willing to try. I bit my lip and kept my naughtiness silent.

"Where are we going now?"

"You said you wanted to see what made me tick, right?"

A grin curled my lips, my eyes narrowed.

"So stop asking so many questions and follow me."

The ring of laughter erupted before I could stop it. "So this how you spend your Friday night's, luring women up into your lair and taking them on a wild goose chase to keep them confused?"

He let loose his own bout of laughter but soon quieted. "No, far from it, I don't...I don't entertain much. Normally, I won't allow anyone past the office."

My eyes swept over the room behind me as I left it behind. "No one?"

"No one," he said calmly turning to stand in front of another sliding door, "If you haven't noticed, I'm a bit of an introvert—one that likes to pretend that I'm not. Saves me answering a lot of useless questions that I don't care to answer."

Seriously strange, I thought but pressed on. "Then why on earth am I here?"

"Curiosity."

Walking towards him as he still stood in front of the pocket door, and looking so damn hot right now I couldn't care less about his oddities. It was kind of flattering that I was the first company allowed in—if in fact, he was not a bold face liar...or a really smooth player. But what would I know about players? I have only observed them from a distance. I was never in league with their targeted prey.

"Okay." I drug the word out slowly, giving my head a shake.

"And to help me open doors." He gave me a wink. "Would you mind sliding the door open for me?"

"Sure," I laughed with a raised brow, "that's what I am here for."

"Exactly."

"You do know what they say about curiosity, don't you?"

"Yes, but then where would the world be without it?" His answer was cute but something flashed in his eyes that I couldn't quite register—something dark, only for a minute then it was gone.

I nodded in agreement, letting go of whatever I had seen in his eyes. Everyone has ghosts in the shadows. Who was I to go digging up their graves?

I brushed by him, my shoulder touching the soft blue cotton of his shirt and barely reaching the protruding muscles of his well-maintained pectorals. The low thudding boom of the music downstairs vibrated through the floor as the song changed—thankfully, it hid the low whimper that escaped me as I touched him.

I pulled at the edge of the door and it easily gave way into another dark room. This time the colouring was different, hues of reds and near violets scatter across the ceiling like perfectly placed starlight. I stepped into it. My jaw came unhinged. Spectral lights brightened and revealed row upon row of painted canvas all stacked together on light wooden easels.

Chapter 13

What in the world?

My eyes were fixed on them. Their vibrant colours drew my soul as their stories sang out. I edged closer toward them, peeking over my shoulder at my host only for a moment—seeing that slight of unreadable emotion in his eyes, and then turned back to the coloured pieces of his soul.

"Did you paint these?"

He strolled by me and set the platter down on a short table centred at the other end of the room, then moved to stand beside me. "Do you like them?"

"Oh my...yes, they are beautiful." My fingers reached to touch them but I drew them back in. "And so...what is the word I am looking for?"

"Dark?"

My eyes rushed to him, and I shook my head. "Well, maybe just a bit. But no, that is not the word I was thinking of." A hush of silence took over the room as the muffled thrum of the music below became more muted than it was before. Chills ran across my arm and drew my eyes down to where Shayne touched it with the side of the opened bottle of water.

"Thanks," I whispered, taking it from him and turned back to the art.

"These are magnificent," I hummed strolling past him and moving onto the next painting, then the next, and the next, seeing so much of who he must be. So many emotions thrust upon a blank canvas, hungry to transform into something tangible, to be more than just a memory set to drift upon the wind.

"You truly like them?"

"Yes," I hummed glancing up at him, feeling him draw nearer.

He grinned, dragging his teeth across his bottom lip. Tilting his head to the right—something feral harbouring in his eyes, he whispered, "They pale in comparison to real living works of art."

I huffed out a nervous laugh, wrinkling my nose not truly understanding his meaning and turned to face him, finding him studying me with sharp eyes.

"I need to see you in the light," he said holding his hand out for me to take.

With narrowed eyes, I slowly clasped hold of his large hand and let him tow me behind him.

Taking no more than five steps and pushing open a door, he swiped his hand over a switch nearly blinding us both in light then turned to me.

"May I touch your face?"

The tenderness in his voice washed away the art, the colours, all of what he had created and opened up to me. It became only about the man standing beside me, watching me.

This must be some kind of artist thing, I told myself—a muse of sorts that he used to spark his artistic creations.

"Yes," I whispered swallowing hard, my insides trembling and on fire.

He stepped in front of me, hands lifting slowly, fingers grazed across the edge of my jaw. As his eyes watched me, with something so raw and so animalistic in them, I didn't know whether to run away or let him draw me deeper into his magical strangeness.

He gently removed the cold bottle of water from my fingers and set it on the edge of one of the counter nearby, then quickly brought it back and placed it on the other side of my face—his thumb slowly tracing a line across my cheekbone.

His gaze sharpened, studying something only he could see in my eyes. I pressed my face into his touch. The heat of his flesh against mine prickled and burned at the same time, and I lifted my hand to touch his.

"May I touch your lips?"

"Yes," I breathed out, my body unsteady now.

His thumb left behind its slow caress of my jaw and found its way to the dip above my mouth. So gentle at first, I could barely feel it. Exploring the plump fullness of my bottom lip, his tender touch slid along the curve of it, while his other hand gently cupped the edge of my jaw.

I looked up at him as he touched me, daring to see into his soul just as he was studying mine.

"May I taste the sweetness of your flesh?"

Something so wild and untamed burned through me, cutting off every ounce of connection to the logical part of my brain that screamed to say no—choking that bitch into silence as she dared to remind me about someone else.

What about Jeremy? It tried to say, *what about…*

He leaned in, his mouth close to mine.

"What about whom?" I breathed out.

He hesitated. "What?"

Burning in the heat his closeness, I shut down my inner voice of reason and whispered, "Yes."

Both of his hand raised to the sides of my face, slipping just until his fingers lingered along the back of my head, tipping my face upwards, his lips grazed mine—breathing me in. My head pulled against his hands. My mouth opened to greet his but his hands held me still. His lips were merely a tease of flesh, not pressing onto mine, leaving me wanting—sliding down the edge of my jaw.

Widened his mouth, Shayne's breath grew hot against the hollowed dip of my neck. A whimper escaped me but I didn't care if he heard me or not. This time it was nearing torture what he was doing.

Oh my gaud, what was he doing?

My mind whirled as he held me in restraint, his lips no more than ghosts upon my flesh. Teeth grazed over my tender skin, goosebumps flared over my bare arm as he bared his teeth and bit gently into the curve of my neck. I couldn't stop the moan, no more than I could stop my panties from growing more damp.

His hands slipped down around my back and held me firmly against his bite. I arched, exposing more of my neck—breasts swelled painfully against my tight shirt as his tongue licked at the tenderness that was left by his teeth. Gentle fingers lowered down along the side of my hips and cupped my backside, lifting me to his groin—gently moving us forward to set me on the counter—my back to the mirror. Hands still firm on my hips, he held me into the heat of his groin.

Wrapping my hands around his neck for support, I felt the tightness in his muscles when he moved. Face to face, we stayed—not breathing for a moment, seeing each other in the light. A wry pull on his full mouth curled while hands slowly ran up the back of my spine, fingertip to fingertip.

"You are magnificent."

My heart stopped hearing his strange words, and lost to find words of my own.

Shayne's eyes broke their intense dance with mine as he leaned back and I could breathe again. Heat, where the wetness between my legs was press against him, sweltered as he grew harder. I wanted to reach out, to grip hold of his hips, and press him into me but he spoke so softly that I lost my courage.

"Will you wear something for me?"

I bit my bottom lip—staring into his blue icy pools and nodded. Not caring what it was he wanted me to put on as long as he touched me.

His hands left my sides and found the top button of his shirt. Slowly he unbuttoned each one—never wavering from his mission. Button by button, the hard curves of his chest and the rippled muscles of his stomach were exposed as the shirt came undone.

My libido spiralled out of control at the sight of him undressing in front of me. Finishing his last button, he removed the shirt and layed it on the edge of the counter next to me and leaned in, pressing against me.

A soft moan escaped me as he lowered his hands to wedge themselves over mine—breath to breath, feeling the heat of his lips so close but not touching.

"Can I take off your shirt?" His voice was low and sultry as he spoke.

I couldn't find my voice. It was gone—lost in my breathlessness. I could only nod as I arched my back, allowing him access—the fullness of my breasts aching.

He lowered his mouth to the edge of my ear and inhaled, while his nimble strong fingers found the front of my shirt and undid the top button—pulling at the edges of my shirt, button by button, to reveal more of my chest. His palms grazed deliberately over the top of my nipples, making them hard and stand at attention while a quiver ran through my legs.

The next button came undone as he pulled the cloth wide, grazing over the hardness of my nipples once more.

Gaud, his slowness was so sensual, so controlled, and absolutely driving me crazy. I bit hard into my lip. A distraction from the painful pleasure his touch was giving me—and the terrible state my panties were now in.

Glancing back up, an impish smirk held my eyes as he slid his hands down to the last button and pulled it back—opening it wide. His fingers lifted, hovering over the front lock of my bra.

"Can I take this off?"

"Yes," I whispered softly in a long exhale, desperate for him to lay his hands on me—to feel the heat of his hand on me.

Both hands rose to cup a breast, letting the fullness rest within his palms and pinching the nipples lightly—making me gasp in his teasing and making them poke out—paining as they fought against the soft cloth holding them in.

"Fuck," I breathed out, as he slid the bottom of my bra up letting my fullness fall out and harden as they dropped.

Abandoning my breasts, his fingers slid down scooping around my backside and pulled me into the warm, hard bulge that had grown big enough to fill out the folds in his pleated pants.

I heard him unleash a rumble in his throat, gritting his teeth—fighting back something, as he ground gently into me. I moaned again. My stomach tightened, needing to press back against his hardness just to ease the tender pain that had grown between my legs.

He eased off just a bit then inhaled and returned to my shirt, pulling the edges of it down over my shoulders. Undoing the front of my bra and slid the straps down my shoulders.

Pulling me into him, Shayne took my arms the rest of the way out of my dark clothing then picked up his from the counter and slid it over me, replacing my shirt with his.

As I slid into it, the smell of him wrapped around me—making the pulse between my legs more palpable, beating harder and harder. Fingers lowered to the top of my jeans and unbuttoned them, slowly pulling the zipper down. His finger slipped lower across the front and pushed in.

Fuck, fuck, I exhaled the words silently in my head.

Gripping both sides of my hips, he slid me further back onto the countertop. "Lift up for me."

Pressing my hands hard against the cold marble counter, I raised my backside up and he pulled at the sides of my jeans, edging them down around the curve of my hips and sliding them over my feet. He stepped away only long enough to remove me from my pants, dropping them on the floor and return to his previous position—still enlarged and solid as he pressed hard against my white cotton panties now soaked because of his teasing.

He rocked into me, keeping me tight against him—his need for me now solid as it moved on its own.

His hands slid away from my hips and move along the edges of the blue shirt I was now wearing and murmured, "I knew it would look good on you." His words sounded breathy and rough as if he was caught somewhere between desire and pain.

"Um," I whispered shyly, biting my lip, "I am feeling a little bit underdressed."

"Is that so? Well, we can't have that now, can we?"

I bit harder on the edge of my bottom lip and shook my head no, then moved, trying to slide off the counter to help him undress. But his hands moved too quick and gently pressed me back.

"Don't move."

Shayne's eyes flared then narrowed, his nimble fingers lowered undoing the catch on his pleated pants, popping the button and pulling the fly open then Shayne pulled at the edges of the grey cloth, widening the opening and revealing the hard flesh it had held inside.

Sweet mother of...fuck.

The thickness of his girth pushed tight against his dark blue boxers—the plump tip of his penis peeking daringly out over the edge of the elastic band.

My innards clenched and I drew in my breath seeing the massive size of him now almost visible. My body shook releasing wild butterflies to wreak havoc on my innards, caught somewhere between awe and fear of his manhood.

I have never had anything that big anywhere near my vagina.

He must have seen the fear in my eyes at seeing him.

"Don't worry, I'm not as scary as I seem. We won't do anything until you say yes," Shayne whispered, "okay?"

Gaud, who was this man? I nodded again.

"Say it."

"Okay." I breathed out as Shayne slowly moved toward me and pressed the hard ready part of him up against me once more.

Chapter 14

His fingers gently slid down the edge of the shirt, resting on the outside of each breast, letting my nipples show. He leaned down and ran his tongue lightly over one, then moved to the other, all the while slowly, rocking against my wetness.

So slow, he was so damn slow—controlled about everything—even his breathing was tempered as he moved his hands over me. My head rocked back as his mouth claimed my right nipple. Pinching his lips around it then opening his mouth wide, the heat of his tongue lapped up the tender edge—flicking it before he pulled away and blew air over the wetness his mouth had left behind.

Fuck.

Returning to the other side, mirroring his efforts, he laid a large warm hand in between the rises of my chest. The heat of his skin on mine sent chills through me as he swept fingers to trace down the slope of my breast, across my navel and over the top of my panties. I rolled my head forward and opened my eyes, only to see *his* roaming over my body.

Lifting his gaze he stared into me, eyes dilated.

"What are we doing Mr. Matthews?" I breathed out slow and wanting, just as his fingers breached the inside of my thighs—tracing the seam of my soaked underwear.

"Being curious, Miss Morrison."

"Mmm," Was all I could say as finger left the seam and fell beneath the cloth, stroking the hot wet opening between my legs. Slowly, oh my gaud, so damn slow he touched—sliding his large finger deeper into my heat. Then pulled it out to add another, then another, filling me just with his touch, driving me closer to a place I had only read about in books or seen in the movies.

I let go of my restraint and pushed against his fingers. My eyes wanting to close as tension began to deepen.

"Open your eyes, Miss Morrison," Shayne hummed, "don't hide your excitement where I can't see it."

Such a strange requested but I did as he said. I lowered my gaze, seeing the glistening on those big long fingers as he stroked me in and out.

My breath quickened. My insides tightened on his touch, closing in on ecstasy just as he pulled his fingers out and left me wanting.

"Not yet," he whispered, leaning in. His mouth hot against my neck—letting my engines cool down, "I want you to feel the pull of longing everywhere. I want you to see the true colours of your desire but you're not ready yet." His mouth traced down along my collarbone, his breath hot against my raging body. Licking and blowing as his mouth explored the taste of my skin.

He leaned back and reached under the counter for a minute, and pulled two thick towels out, tucking them in behind my back. Gently, Shayne curled his strong fingers around my sides and ran along the curve of my ribs. Slipping them under the fullness of my breast again, cupping them, his thumb teased the fully erect tender nipples.

"Lie back," he coaxed soft and hungry to see all the curves of my torso undressed by the overhead light. I lowered my back onto the softness of the towels and watched the fires burn in his eyes. His breath caught in his lungs while his hands ran back down the sides of my ribs and across my navel then slid them under me, pulling up on my lower back and making the arch in my spine more defined—torso muscles tight just above my hips.

A low growl rumbled in his throat as he pressed himself hard up against me and soothed some of the pain throbbing in both of us.

His hand left my side and slid down the hollow of my hip. I followed the pressure of it as it found the edge of my white underwear and skated over the top, grazing the wet damp cloth. Pressing his manhood hard against me, Shayne moved his thumb up and down the wet valley of cloth. The song of my torment building again as he continued his exploring.

"Fuck," I swore with a rushed breath, the heat in my body nearing consumption, "I don't do this kind of thing. This wasn't in my plans. I wasn't expecting to take off my panties until I showered."

"Well, technically, we are in the bathroom if it makes you feel any better."

Gaud that voice, I thought. It was as warm and rich as melted butter.

"And who said anything about taking them off."

His fingers slipped in under the hem of my wet panties and pushed through to the other side—rubbing a bent knuckle up into the deepest part of my wetness, coaxing, taunting then clutched the cloth in his fist and pulled it to the side.

Lowering, he ran his thick strong tongue down through my dark hair that peeked out from under the bunched cloth. Making the muscle pointed and hard—lunging it inward—he buried his face into me.

Oh Fuck, Fuck, Fuck. Everything scorched and shuddered.

Dragging his thick pink muscle back up through my dark wet hair, he slowly rose, eyes narrowed and wild—his mouth, serious as he licked the taste of me off of his lips.

He drew in a deep breath. The taut muscles that painted his torso, tightened as he pressed the edge of his penis up against my exposed vagina, now dripping with desire.

Over and over he rubbed the bulbous tip—ribbed, hard and blushing, letting the length of him drag over my sensitive opening.

Mother fucker, what was I doing?

I don't have sex with strangers.

I barely had sex with Jeremy. *Fuck, fuck, fuck.*

How the hell did I get in this position? Fuck.

I groaned, wanting him so badly. His penis, now fully exposed, free from the cloth of his boxers, rubbing hard against me had freed it. It was so deliciously big that all I could think of was how it would feel deep inside of me—touching every aching nerve that was screaming for attention—never wanting anyone so badly in my life. What was he waiting for?

I watched his veined hard member throb as it touched me, glistening more and more as it rubbed against the juices of my excitement.

"We don't have to do this." His voice was so soft, lips full as he spoke. Even though Shayne's words were soft and controlled his body tremored with anticipation. "We won't take it any further until you tell me yes."

Shayne rubbed against me once more. Holding my underwear to the side with one hand and the other gently holding my hips in place to keep me from moving, he kept all the tension between us firm.

I exhaled. *Fuck. It's crazy. It's insane. It's not who you were this morning but sweet mother of...I let my inhibitions go and dove deep into his icy blue eyes, letting his magic swirl through me.*

What was I waiting for?

"Yes." The word slipped over my tongue. It was so small yet held so much power.

"You're sure."

Was I?

This was my chance to say no. To give him back his soft blue shirt and gather my senses about me and my clothes and get back to where I was supposed to be mingling with potential clients and knowledge seekers as I had planned.

He said it was up to me.

I had the power to call it all off.

I exhaled and prepared myself to answer him.

Say no, say no, say no.

"Yes," I breathed out—"I'm sure."–shutting off the boring logical part of me that still was fighting to protect me from this illogical curious game we were playing. Nodding, keeping his gaze, I pressed my hands hard against the marble counter, forcing my vagina harder onto his slow thrust—to let all of the magic of his touch drown me in this strange river of spells he had cast on me.

The tip of his manhood slid up, disappearing into the fold between my legs, and pressed past the cloth of my underwear, filling the entry of my aching hole.

A loud exhale escaped me as I took all of him.

Gaud he felt so good.

But he pulled out again, resting his large beast on the edge of my pubic bone, throbbing in his excitement.

Shayne leaned to the side, hauling out a drawer and rummaged through it. Exhaling, his fingers explored the innards looking for something, as he pursed his lips. Then his mouth straightened, flicking his brow at me, his fingers ending their search and pulled out a small square package.

Bringing it to meet his impish grin, he bit the edge and ripped the rest of the package away.

I reached out, slow and cautious, grabbing the rounded soft Playtex ring, taking it from him. "Can I touch you?" I whispered softly, playing by the same rules as he seemed to be.

This was a game of permissions—a game of slow and precise movements, reminding me of chess in a way. Taking down the opponents forces until they had no more moves to play.

He exhaled a breathy laugh, making his smile less intimidating and more boyish, lopsided and playful.

"Yes," he moaned softly, letting his hands drop to the sides of my hips, regaining the wild intense hunger in his eyes.

Removing the tender rubber from its sheath and setting it aside, I laid the broadside over the top of the eye of his manhood. The hard rod twitched at my touch on its own accord and then once more as I slid my fingers down along the side, rolling the rim over the thick muscle now pulsing in my hands. I pushed with more pressure, trying to force it down, not entirely sure it was big enough to fit over him.

But with a little patience it finally did.

Finding the base, a loud groan came from Mr. Matthews. His back arched, the firm roundness of his muscular backside clenched and the long smooth muscles that ran from his abdomen down into the beautiful v defined his groin. Shayne pressed his long hard muscle back against my hands, now snuggled into the safety shield.

"Ready?" he whispered.

Oh, fuck yes. My animal instincts screamed silently in my head but I only whispered back a soft slow 'yes.'

His thick fingers moved to find the folds of my wetness and pressed in, slowly he counted with his fingers, one, then two then three, in and out until my muscles relaxed on his touch—learning the thickness of his fingers as he moved in and out with slow hard circles inside of me.

My breath sped up in shorter inhales as the tension of my loins grew hot again. I watched him as he watched us growing hotter together.

A low rumbling groan filled his throat, his pain of needing my wetness all around him becoming too much, knowing my answer was yes. He pulled his fingers out, glistening with my readiness, then wet the top and sides of his covered throbbing muscle with it—preparing it for the journey, and saving me some uncomfortable friction.

His fingers left his rod then rose to his nose. He inhaled my scent, licking the rest of me from him.

Fuck, fuck, fuck. I groaned inside. His eyes grew feral as his hand lowered and found me dripping wet again.

He bit the edge of his full bottom lip, pressed forward, groaning so loud that he nearly drown out the thudding base that had changed from a slow thud to a savage pounding rhythm as if on cue.

Fingers, that left me wanting, were soon replaced by the full tip of him filling the void. Slowly, inch by inch, he pressed inward then pulled out. Again and again, he moved gently, letting my heat adjust to his massive size—learning his hardness, and letting my body welcome him with its sweet slippery juices.

The aching stopped stinging but turned into something else, something animalistic as he continued to enter and pull out. Gripping the side of my hips, he pulled me forward—holding me in place as he sped up his thrusts. Dragging his thumb down over the top of my vulva as he pressed further into me.

Everything slowed.

My breath, my thoughts, the way my body pushed against his as he moved in and out—deliberate and precise, so all my insides felt the full length of him every time.

My mind swam in strange colours.

His eyes examined me, keeping me spellbound in his magic, watching his muscles ripple and move in the shadows the light cast down over his moving torso.

Burning sweetly with his thrusts, my insides tightened on him. Even from within the protective sheath, I felt the throb of his largeness taking me somewhere I had never been before. I looked down and watched as our bodies crashed together, the faint lines of his veins as they disappeared deeply into my dark wet hair.

The rush of seeing him enter me over and over again, sent my excitement into another level of fire.

Fuck, fuck, fuck.

I had to look away.

My mind was not able to make my eyes work and rolled them back in my head. I couldn't breathe. I couldn't think. I couldn't do anything but rise to meet his hard thrusting touch.

Leaned back against the cushion of towels, clutching them hard within my fisted fingers, I climbed higher and higher. My body tightened and shook. Not able to stop it, I let it go and cried out as my body convulsed with a tidal wave of pleasure all over his thrusting sword.

I was not alone.

Deep thrusts continued faster and faster until he loosened his own joy in our feverous game. Driving hard and fast his eyes flared as his release came in a loud growl and shudders surged through his body until he let go, falling forward on top of me.

Shayne's hot breath across my skin kept my sensitive nipple erect. His moans of approval as he kissed the edge of it, surely meant that in our strange game of chess, he had killed my queen and took no prisoners.

Fuck, fuck, fuck that was so…

"Are you hungry?"

His head lifted from the nestle spot between my breast and stared down at me—his mouth sweet, and his eyes soft.

"Yes."

Chapter 15

We sat in the middle of his bed, just to the side of his art room, him still in his boxers, and me still in his shirt, and drank our lukewarm Perrier as we ate the bits of meat and cheese he had brought in earlier before we got *curious.*

With the heat of tension lulled from our extreme chess game, the conversation was easier and surprising in its own measure.

"Do you have any of your paintings in Galleries?" I asked shoving a piece of cheese in my mouth, looking back over at the canvases that leaned against the wall on the other side of the room.

"No," he said low and docile, "I don't paint for others, only for me."

"Oh, I didn't mean..." My words cut off, seeing that strange look in his eyes again, wondering if it was sadness that dwelled there.

"It's okay." He laughed, lying back on the bed, stretching his arms out over his head behind him. "I paint to express my emotions. It's cheaper than going to see a shrink to deal with my inner demons."

I looked back over to the paintings and nodded, stuffing another piece of cheese in my mouth. Shayne was not only smart and money conscious, I came to the conclusion that he might be sweet and sensible as well.

"How do you handle your stress?" he hummed leaning up on his elbow and staring at me with big blue eyes, his hair a chaotic sexy mess.

My heart thrummed in my chest, feeling something shift again in the air with his tone.

"Hmm, well…I guess I throw myself into my career."

"Not always a healthy choice you know."

"I know, but it's different for me," I said, leaning back on my elbow mirroring his pose. "I've spent most of my life being and doing, what everyone else needed me to be or wanted me to be. And it nearly smothered me." I picked at the edge of the platter, staring into the soft curve of its design. "But now…I don't. Or at least I am trying not to. I am doing what I need to do in order to find me—to make my life as it should be. No more walking in other's shadows or dancing to the beat of their drums…I make my own music and dance in front of the world singing out the lyrics to the songs I wrote—hoping someone else might find it inspiring and become brave enough to sing their own song."

I finished and glanced up at him, seeing his stare intense and turn a bit hungry again. "So, I live and breathe, and dive into my work because it saves me—a well of hope so to speak."

Shayne grinned and sat up, sliding the platter of food onto the floor then turned back to me, his grin gone. His hand brushed against my cheek, tucking a loose strand of hair behind my ear and stilled. His eyes narrowed, breath hitched in his lungs as he turned away and dug for something in the nightstand beside the big bed.

Moving around to the end of the bed, he lowered onto his knees, then laid a large pad of paper with a dozen pencils—a smorgasbord of colours and sizes down on the twisted sheets.

"What on earth are you doing now?" I laughed.

"Don't move," he whispered fevered, wildness flared in his eyes as his hands picked up one of the pencils and started to scratch at the paper in front of him.

"What are you doing?"

"Creating."

"Can I ask what?"

"You," he finally grinned again, looking up at me and tucked one of the pencils behind his ear.

My heart panged with fear. He can't be serious. I glanced nervously around the room then back at him again.

Shayne rose to his feet and headed towards the rows of coloured canvases looking for something. Standing with his hands on his hips, his glutes twitched within the shadows under his boxers as he turned this way and that in his mad search. Leaning down and pulling something from behind one of the paintings, he picked it up and placed it on his face.

"So this is what you do? You bring random girls home, get them undressed, and draw them?" I said half teasingly. I hadn't actually seen any paintings of naked girls in the collection by the wall but for all I knew, he might keep those tucked somewhere else.

Turning back to me, his eyes framed in black, Shayne gave me a strange glare. "No," he said, falling back to his knees and began scratching again at the paper, "Miss Morrison, nothing I have done in the last few hours, since I saw you up on that stage, has been 'normal' for me."

His eyes only skirted up at me for no more than a breath.

"Oh," I said feeling a bit presumptuous for saying something that sounded maybe just a bit cruel.

He sank down, hurriedly getting lost in his sketching. I watched him drift somewhere far away from here—somewhere only he knew how to find, where the colours of the world spoke to those who knew how to listen.

I twisted my mouth, feeling just a bit self-conscious as he glanced up at me continually briefly, then back down to his paper.

"Can I see?"

"Nope," he breathed out, flicking his brow and actually looking at me for more than just a second, pulling the paper towards him and pulling the edge of it closer to him so I couldn't peek. "Not until I have the shape of you figured out."

So I sat picking at the tray and watched, letting him find *the shape of me.*

"Hmm," he hummed, looking up at me but still absorbed in his faraway world, making some last scratches—using the coloured sticks this time then put them down. "It's not what it could be—only a quick imprint of what I see when I look at you."

"Show me," I said, smiling meekly, a bit terrified really of wondering how I looked through his eyes—knowing after what we had been up to, I probably looked a fright.

I saw the slight tremor of his hands as he turned the pad around slowly. "I don't normally show anyone these, so..."

My hand lifted to my mouth and I gasped. "Shayne, it's beautiful. The sketch, I mean, not...me."

I glanced at him, his mouth a bit more relaxed than it had been before, and the blue of his icy irises deepened. The darkness was there again as he watched me, touching the edges of his soul. I don't know how in such a short time, he captured so much depth in just scratches of colour. I'm not sure if this is how I actually looked in real life, but through his eyes, I was...beautiful.

"You seriously should do something with your work, you're so talented."

He crept towards me and gently removed the thick pad of paper from my hands, dropping it over the side of the bed. His mouth severe, ajar just enough to see the perfect line of white teeth pressed against his full pink lips. On all fours, stopping only inches from where I sat he breathed out, "Can I touch you again?"

And he did, sweet mother of...did he ever.

This time there was no slowness in his touch, it was hard and fast.

His body so ridged and firm against mine—thrusts deeper and claiming as they brought me into his colours of life. I tried to kiss his hungry mouth but he only let his lips graze over mine, pulling them away to slide over my neck, my breasts and further down where he masterfully brought me into a rage of fire once more.

This strange dance between us went on even after the thrum of the bass below in his nightclub quieted and the absence of bodies long departed the premises.

This dance, wild and gentle, sweet and raw, was built of the hungers that we both held within and burned for what seemed like hours until we finally culled it into a passive lull.

I closed my eyes and let this strange man's arms wrap around me, holding me safely against his stomach.

I knew this wasn't love.

I knew this was nothing of the sort, but for me, it was the closest I had ever been to guessing what it must feel like.

Letting the slow rhythm of his breath wash over me, I exhaled one last breath before fading into sleep.

"Happy Birthday, Andy."

Chapter 16

The sound of life stirring outside an open window brought me into consciousness, my eyes heavy as they opened. Not recognizing the space I was in right away, glancing around the room I gasped as reality kicked in.

Everything I did, everything I let happen, everything I said he could do to me sent shocks of utter disbelief through me, pulling me into full alertness as I remembered him.

My nose wrinkled as I narrowed my eyes, slowly turning onto my back and peeked over my shoulder. Blowing out a loud puff of air, I let myself breath again seeing the empty space on the bed beside me and the note on the pillow with a set of keys on the top of it.

Leaning on my elbow, I reached for the paper, looking around the room.

Sorry I didn't wake you but I had to leave,
Something came up.
Take the car back to the hotel,
and just leave the keys at the front desk.
S.M

'Hmm.' Was all I could say. What else could I say?
It was what it was—a one-night-stand, a wonderfully hot and crazy one night stand.

Everyone has done it.

Everyone has got caught up in the heat of the moment.

"Everyone but me," I sighed, grabbing the keys and got out of bed to try to find my clothes.

*

Pulling into the hotel parking lot, I pulled the black Beemer warily into one of the spots far in the back, careful to keep it far away from the other vehicles. I locked the door and walked back to the lobby with my head up, shoulders back, and ready to start the day. But each step made me feel dirty, definitely needed a shower and a change of clothes. I might have driven a BMW back to my hotel but in spite of that, it was still a walk of shame that I was doing, no matter how I got there.

Fuck it, suck it up.

At least it wasn't with some loser that I couldn't remember the name of, drunk at a bar. I had only been there done that once, a long time ago. Ugh. This guy at least was super-hot, super-smart and to top it off, super-rich. Maybe a dick for running off, mind you, but hey I could have done worse.

Striding into the lobby, I marched toward the front desk and handed the girl an envelope marked 'Mr. S. Matthews' and wondered how many times this had happened before.

"This is for Mr. Matthews," I said, trying not to turn red, knowing exactly what was in there.

"Oh, of course, I'll see that he gets it."

A lovely paled hair girl quickly took up the envelope and placed it under the counter. Thanking her, I quickly looked away before guilt of my sins could flush my cheeks any more than they already had, and glanced up at the clock.

It was Ten o'clock.

I had just enough time to grab a quick shower and a change of clothes before the first lecture and put all of this lustful non-sensible business behind me. My face burned remembering a slightly stimulating position I had been in just a few hours ago. "Ugh, this is going to harder than I thought," I uttered, shaking my head I marched to the elevator and pressed the button.

*

Fifteen minutes later, I hit the lobby again. Walking down the hall and heading towards the opened door to the conference, I filed in behind all the other folks that were just getting there. Sliding in along the wall, I settled into the seat I had yesterday and smiled at Mrs. Ferguson as she greeted me quietly.

"Oh, good morning, dear. Did you have a fun night?"

My eyes widened, all my guilt of naughty doings painting a rosy hue across my cheeks as my heart almost stopped.

"I left early before the meet and greet was over," she said, "Headache and all. Everyone looked to be having a good time."

I exhaled, breathing again. She didn't know. Of course she didn't know what I did. How could she?

Chill out, Andy.

"Yes, it was very nice, thank you."

"That's wonderful, you looked like you were having fun when I left," she finished, smiling at me then turned toward the stage as the timekeeper stepped out from the tall dark curtains and announced the first speaker of the day.

Good, this was good.

Back on track and ready to take notes. *Notes?* "Damn it." I cursed under my breath.

"What is it, dear?"

"I forgot my note pad."

She smiled and hurriedly grabbed something from her purse. "No worries, dear," she said, handing me a clean pad of paper and a pen. "I carry extras at these things. Always be prepared I say, would you care to use one?"

"Oh, that is so nice of you, thank you." I smiled, taking the paper and pen from her then turned to focus on the large jolly looking man now on the stage as he began to speak.

With my head now cleared and engaged, I scratched down some really great points on time management and the importance of small sprints of concentrated working shifts. Excellent little tidbits for getting more work done while avoiding burning yourself out trying to do everything at once.

My excitement reeled about me and mixed with the crowd's enthusiastic energy that buzzed in high waves about the room. *At least the weekend wouldn't be a complete right off,* I thought, scolding myself again for being so foolish and acting like a teenage school girl over a boy, no less.

I already had a boy...well a man, sort of...I think.

A man with hands that were cold and shaky. And his emotional contribution to our lovemaking, if that is what you could call it, was less than inspired. It was more along the lines of a 'wham-bam-thank you ma'am,' get it over quickly, so he could go back to his computer or games or work or whatever the hell it was he did on that thing all night.

It was nothing compared to what had transpired between Mr. Matthews and I. His touch was so soft and gentle—hands, warm like fire that blazed over my skin in a slow burn. Tingles spread over my arms giving me goosebumps just thinking about it, warming places down below.

This was ridiculous.

I shook my head, trying to clear the thought of Shayne Matthews away just as something touched the side of my arm, making me jump. I turned towards it to find ice blue eyes staring back at me, burning into me, bright with stardust against the dark night.

"I think you dropped this, Miss Morrison."

Shayne's lips curled as he handed me a folded piece of paper then rose and walked away. I turned, my eyes following him as he slowly marched to the back of the room—watching the muscles in his body move with precision, packaged dangerously within a dark maroon coloured dress shirt and a black leather belt that held his charcoal pleated pants just right.

Fuck.

My eyes undressed him as he moved, making me ache in remembrance of what he was capable of doing to me, caught in a trance of last night's fever. He paused at the exit and glanced back at me over his shoulder. His eyes wild as his mouth curved into a wickedly impish crook.

My gaud, he was sexy.

He disappeared out the door and I hurried back to the paper he had placed in my hand.

Ditch this crowd.

Come play hooky with me.
I'll be waiting out back in the car.

My loins tightened and burned. An internal fire, from instant lust thinking of his hands all over me, heated my body and I exhaled a little too loudly.

Oh my fuck! What is this man doing to me?

"Are you alright dear?" Mrs. Ferguson announced, looking at me, worry in her eyes as she interrupted my secret moment. "You look a little flushed."

"Oh, I'm, Um…"

What am I doing? What the fuck am I doing?

"I'm, ah…not feeling that well."

Yes, you are, you are fine. Just sit your skinny ass down and leave that man alone.

"I think I'm going to get some air."

"Aw, you poor thing, probably something that's going around no doubt." She smiled, patting me on the arm. "Don't you worry, dear. I'll take notes for you."

"Oh my, you are just so sweet," I said, feeling just a wee bit guilty, "Thank you, Mrs. Ferguson."

"Judy," she said smiling.

"What?"

"You can call me, Judy," she continued, waving me away with her free hand probably hoping to move me away before she caught whatever it was that I had, "Now you go on, take care of yourself."

"Thank you," I replied, turning and walking just a little too quickly toward the exit. Not knowing who I was, not recognizing the path I was on. Not looking behind me, just as he had, I walked out the exit and headed straight for the back parking lot.

Chapter 17

I strode out the front door and around the back, nervous, excited and completely out of my mind.

But there he stood...bigger than life. His mouth wide and smug like he was a cat that was just about to swallow the canary...and oh, did I mention, hot, hot, hot?

Just looking at him as he rolled up the sleeves of his dress shirt made my panties wet again. The defined curves in his forearm shadowing its magnificence as it moved.

A queer grin painted my mouth, as I neared Shayne's car. I flexed my fingers in my angst of this un-Andy like rendezvous I had been invited into. Almost there, my toe caught on a loose pebble causing me to stumble. He rushed forward, grabbing for my arm, and caught before I face planted into the back of his black Beemer.

Pulling me into him—into his subtle but intoxication aroma, my chest rested against his torso as he spoke, "Are you alright?"

"Yeah, I'm fine."

"Good," he said lowering his hand and curling his fingers around the edge of my backside, letting them touch in between my cheeks.

Fuck... just fuck.

"Get in," he whispered into my ear, "We're going site seeing." He moved back and opened the door wide for me to get in then ran around to the other side, starting the engine.

"Where are we going?"

"Site seeing...like I said."

He peeked over at me with a crooked grin, driving us out of the parking lot and down into the city. Making a quick right turn, he pulled into another parking lot just on the edge of the bay.

Shayne glanced down at his Rolex. "Hurry, the Sea-Demia is about ready to leave."

"What the hell is a 'Sea-Demia'?" I laughed, watching him jump out of his car and run around to the other side, opening my door.

"It's a boat, and if we don't hurry we are going to miss it."

"Okay then."

I glance out over the lot and down to the water's edge. A large thick mast of a boat below towered over the man standing beside it, yelling something into the wind.

The door behind me slammed and Shayne wrapped a large black coat around my shoulders and grinned. "You're going to need this." Grabbing hold of my hand, he grinned and quickly dragged me down the ramp—heading toward the boat bobbing slowly in the ripple of waves and dancing with the wind.

Handing the shouting man what looked like tickets, Shayne edged me forward onto the loading plank, and settled us near the front of the boat, sitting us both down against the side of it.

"Afraid of water?"

I laughed, "A little late now for that question isn't it?"

"Maybe just a bit." He laughed, the corners of his eyes edged with soft lines of humour. "But seriously, are you?"

"No," I breathed out as the boat moved away from the dock. Away from the busy hustle and bustle of the city behind us and into the winds of a changing tide.

My eyes grazed over him as he looked out over the harbour, no doubt seeing all the colours of life within the houses—built in as many shades alongside its high ledged walls. Excitement swirled in my stomach, butterflies and Mexican jumping beans bounced around within my innards. My knees shook and my hands trembled.

Shayne glanced down at me and pulled the coat tighter around my shoulders. "Are you cold?"

I shook my head no but he curled himself around the back of me, covering me with his heat—his body close against my back.

I wasn't cold.

No, this was something else taking hold of me.

Something strong and unspoken.

"Better?"

I nodded, glancing up at him. So tender and sweet—so beautiful and wild that it almost hurt to look at him.

"For a no-nonsense businessman, you are a bit of a bad influence."

"Ah, but I did influence you right?"

"Right."

"Then that's all that matters."

"You're a wicked man, Mr. Matthews."

"Only when I want to be," he chimed in, pressing himself against the back of me. Slipping his hands into the mock pockets of the large black coat he wrapped me in, fingers gripped the edges of my hips—pressing them gently, backing me up to meet snuggly against the front of him.

The boat rocked against the waves cutting its way out through the mouth of the harbour. His fingers wandered deeper and found the zipper of my pants, sliding beneath the cloth and down into the clean, soft hair below.

"We can't do this here," I whisper against his face, now snug against mine.

"Why not?" he hummed back.

Lower and lower, his fingers explored until the fold between my thighs had been discovered.

"Someone will see," I breathed out, barely able to speak as I glanced around the deck, feeling the heat of him inside.

He hushed me with a warm promise. "No, they won't"

My eyes lingered once more on the crowd around us. No one was looking at us—no one.

So relaxing into his touch, I let him do what he wanted. The excitement of being caught just a little thrilling. Slowly, ever so slow he counted inside of me— one finger, then two, then three, dipping in and out as he leaned into my neck. His hot breath against the coolness of the ocean's breath in open sea was mind altering. I groaned more loudly than I realized but my sound was swallowed up by the rushing of waves as they crashed against the sides of the boat.

The vessel rocked with the constant pounding, and I as well as my body quickened with Shayne's counting—of thick fingers covered in my dew as they rushed, in and out, faster and faster as we swept out to sea.

"Oh gaud," I breathed out, clutching at his other hand that was wrapped around my waist holding me still. Closing my eyes to fight the fire just a little longer, just a little more, his teeth bit into the side of my neck and his fingers rushed harder and harder until I could no longer breathe.

Groaning loudly, I moaned my release into the sea.

Not caring if anyone heard me. The sound of my ecstasy washing over me, drowned into the loud echo of passengers as they spied a large iceberg as the boat rounded the bent land.

"Oh, Shayne," I cried again, more softly this time, lifting my hand to rush through his curls at the back of his head. No one was the wiser of our indecent game of counting. Only assuming my shrill cry was that of joy in spotting the large mass of ice floating in the water just like the rest of them.

My eyes slowly opened to the large giant structure of ice that had crested the dark smooth waters of the Atlantic Ocean in front of us.

Drinking everything in, letting the exhilaration of this wildly extraordinary clash of sensations whirl through me, I went again all over his fingers, trembling, tightening against the raw desire of Shayne's touch still moving inside of me.

*

The boat ride back into the harbour was less eventful but just as fun. I watched as his eyes softened to the world around him—how he let himself enjoy the friendly people around him, and the intense way he would look over at me, through breaks in conversation and smile, holding my hand—refusing to let go.

Edging closer to the dock, he wrapped his arms around me, holding me steady in the wake of the large ship against the bobbing shoreline. "You hungry?"

I laughed and squeezed his arms. "Starving."

"Good, I know just the place. I promise it will be better than the pepperoni and cheese platter I fed you this morning."

"I didn't mind."

"I know you didn't but you deserve a better meal than that...since I made you jig class and all."

"Jig?"

A lyrical chime of laughter floated over his beautiful full lips. "It means to skip."

"Ah, well then, Mr. Matthews, I will have you know that you didn't make me *jig*. I'm a big girl you know." I reminded him. "I decided to be bad all on my own."

"You did, did you?"

"Yes," I purred at him, turning to look him straight in the eyes. "Yes."

A low moan escaped him as he pressed himself into me, his largeness already growing. "You keep that up and I might not feed you at all."

I laughed and turned away, walking the plank onto the dock, thinking that would be all right too.

We pulled into the large parking lot, a bright red sign screamed 'Chester's' over the top and I laughed. "Oh my gosh, it's Chester's."

"What? You have had it before?"

"No, it's just something Mrs. Ferguson said about..."

"Who?"

"Judy."

"Who?" he said again.

"No one you know," I said, waving his confusion away, "She mentioned that I needed to try it out before I left the rock."

"Well, whoever Judy is, she's right. I told you we were going to be tourists today, so there is no more reason to come to Saint John's than to eat at Chester's."

We entered the doors and scouted for seats but it was lunch hour. The place was filled to the brim with hungry people. "How about we take it to go?"

I smiled and nodded, looking around at the entertained faces happily dining on their meals. We slowly shuffled our way to the cashier and Shayne ordered us two meals, one of fish and chips the other of clams then made our way to the edge of the building and waited until our number was up.

"Twenty-Three," the young man behind the counter called out.

Leaving me to cut through the crowded line-ups, eyes turned to watch him move. Faces flushed with what I suspected to be dirty thoughts about what they would like to do to him as he passed by those who stood in line waiting for their orders.

Making his way back with a sack full of goodies, some of those eyes lingered back to me, raising brows as he curled his fingers in mine and led me out the door.

My heart sank.

They were right.

I wasn't much to look at. I wasn't a monster by any means but I really didn't look like the kind of girl that one would see attracting a man like him.

He opened the car door for me and I got in, my mouth only a line, and my eyes far away lost in my knowledge.

"What's wrong? Are you alright?"

I sighed and looked up into his bright eyes, and smiled. "Yes, I'm fine just tired I guess."

He smiled back and draped a hand to touch the edge of my chin, brushing a thumb over my bottom lip. "Don't go to sleep on me yet. We're a long way from done."

He really was beautiful.

All the darkness that I saw set in his eye before was gone. I let go of the glances, let go of the doubt that had been installed in me from those few moments inside, and let them all go to hell.

This was about me.

This was about him.

And right now, it was just about us.

He set the take-out bags onto the floor and drove us back to the hotel.

"All done touristing are we?" I asked, biting on my thumb.

Shayne shook his head—curls fell about his face. "Not by a long shot. I just thought maybe we would check out your place."

"It's just a hotel…your hotel. Shouldn't you know what it looks like?"

"I might be part owner of it, but it's not like I have seen the inside of every room or anything."

"Alright," I cooed and shrugged my shoulders, "my place it is."

Chapter 18

Entering in through the back door, Shayne hesitated. "What room are you in?"

"The Marilyn suit."

"Oh, well look at you miss fancy pants. Maybe I should do public speaking more often if it pays that good."

"It was a bump up for losing my reservations. If not we'd already be in my room."

His laughter sang out into the empty hallway, echoing and filling the space with a magic that made me want to just hold him close and drink in his soul.

"I'll meet you there in a minute. No sense in spoiling your reputation by being seen with the likes of me."

"Right," I snickered at him and rolled my eyes.

He only winked at me as I walked past him and through the doors to the lobby. I rounded the corner to the elevators, hoping the doors would open more quickly and held my breath as I slid into the elevator unseen.

Hitting the top button on the panel, I leaned back against the mirrors, riding the cable upward— somewhere mixed between exhaustion, joy, hunger— still wondering what the fuck was I doing.

A ding brought me back, eyes rushing open as I stepped out into the hall. I stopped and grinned then headed toward the tall, dark, beautiful man holding two bags of take-out by my door.

"Okay, smarty pants how did you get up here so fast?"

He pulled out something in his pocket and wagged it around in front of him, grinning from ear to ear. "I have the master key. No stops, no pauses just straight to where I need to go."

"You are just full of surprises aren't you?" I said to him slipping in front of him and sliding my hotel room key through the card reader.

"Maybe," he breathed out, grinning then leaned up against me and let out a low groan.

I couldn't help but feel the heat of his body on mine.

Fuck.

I pushed the door open and he rushed me in, dropping the take-out bags on the floor—guiding us to the right, he pressed me up against the wall. Lowering, Shayne slid his knees in between mine, spreading my legs wide. Hands slid around the curve of my backside and cupped my cheeks pulling me upward onto him, already hard, already wanting to do things to me again.

My hand swung at the door by my head and pressed it hard, opening it as he carried us through the threshold. Setting me down on the countertop, he flicked on the dim lights—eyes wild and dilated.

What was it with countertops? I wondered, then let the thought drift away as he shimmed me out of my pants and undid the front of his.

Fuck.

Shayne's mouth was hungry, teeth grazed against my neck, biting, teasing, as his penis rubbed against my wetness. He pulled away, seeking me out and I open my eyes to see his hunger. "Is it my turn?"

"Yes," I hurried the words out, running my fingers through his loose curls, "Yes, fuck yes."

"Mm, I think I like the way that sounds," he said before his fingers reached for his pocket and ripped open the small square package, not waiting for help from me.

With a loud exhale, he slid the wrapper over his thickness then slid his fingers around the front of my panties, pulling them hard to the side—sliding his fingers into my wet fold then began to count.

One...*gaud.* Two...*oh, gaud*...Three. *Mm, fuck.*

"I also think I like this leave your panties thing on," he growled biting his bottom lip, feeling my body ready for him, pushed himself inside. Not waiting and no slow gentle slides, he wanted me, and the pain on his face showed just how much.

His thumb softly rubbed my clitoris, raising the temperature of my need to match his. I lowered my eyes, watching him enter me, over and over with hunger, his wanting me to feel all of him, needing me to see all of him as he brought me to aroused blindness.

"Fuck," I swore in a low moaning hiss, "Oh, fuck, fuck."

I had to close my eyes.

I had to let go.

He was so hard, so fucking hard. My body felt everything as I came all over him. Again and again, the waves of ecstasy crashed through me, and his over him as his hands clutched harder on my hips thrusting faster and faster until his body shook with violent spasms of release.

"Fuck, Andy, what are you doing to me?" he whispered, so softly that I barely heard it leave his mouth. No, Miss Morrison, but Andy...I came again.

Chapter 19

Stripping down the rest of my clothes I slid open the door to the shower and turned it on, waiting for the water to warm then peeked over my shoulder at him. "Do you want to join me?"

He hesitated just for a breath then nodded. Such a boy he was, all tucked neatly into this beautifully shaped brilliant man body.

We touched in a different manner this time, letting our fingers explore each other's bodies in ways that were not all meant for lustful pleasure but more of seeking out the curves and shadows of how different our bodies were. He reached for a cloth and dabbed some soap on it, gently washing my body, slowly touching me until it ached again.

How can this man make me so damn bothered?

He lingered slowly between my legs, watching me, enjoying how I let myself grind his hand as he cleaned me. His torso grew taught, and his penis climbed upward to touch the edge of his navel. Strong and firm, laced with slender veins as it hardened. Dropping the cloth, he looked at me and I breathed out the words he so desperately needed to hear. Turning me to face the wall, pressing my hands onto the smooth, wet surface, his fingers wedged in mine.

Shayne bent his knees and pressed the hardness throbbing in front of him down the slippery crease of my backside, the curves of my body guiding his.

He gave a slow gentle push, seeking me out, finding his entry and groaned into my ear as he sank himself into me.

Setting my right hand free, he brought his fingers around the front of my stomach and slid them lower as he pushed against me—slipping the palm of his hand down my clitoris, touching it gently but firm enough for me to grind against.

I whimpered out loud.

I let myself become the animal he wanted to feed. Grinding hard into his fingers, and pressing back against his rod, thrusts became harder and harder, while his hand roughly touched where I needed.

Something about the position we were in, sent a wave of different sensations to stir my already spent desire, re-igniting it and sending it spiralling out of control again. I wanted to scream out his name, pull his hair and bite every piece of him as my body tightened and shook.

My fingers, reaching back, clawed into the hard flesh of his ass.

This new world of sexual pleasures was mind-bending and delicious. I ground harder into his fingers—onto his throbbing muscle—never wanting to stop, never wanting to come back down.

My legs wobbled as his last thrusts slowed, he bit hard into the top of my shoulder, pulling me just a little longer into my bliss.

Both of us out of breath—lost somewhere together—we began to laugh, realizing we needed another shower.

Chapter 20

I left him rinsing in the warm running water, jumping out early and hustling to my suitcase to find something comfortable to pull on.

Entering the sitting area, my heart dropped— guilt of what I had been doing these last couple of days, crashing into me. Wildflowers, stuffed into a beautiful bouquet, were set upon my nightstand with a box, wrapped in shiny red paper, tucked underneath.

"Oh, my gaud," I whimpered, hands covering my mouth, now realizing I was a monster, "He remembered."

I had been so angry at my love life that I submerged myself deeply within the man still showering, enjoying our abundant sins of flesh.

So much, I had completely forgotten about Jeremy—left him tucked back in the shadows of my mind and pretended he didn't matter.

What have I done?

I promised myself this weekend, if he cared enough to call—to make any kind of small effort this weekend, I would try to fix this broken link between us—try to make it work.

This was the sign I was hoping for.

I dared to edge near the show of admiration.

I held my breath. My fingers trembled as they touched the soft velvety petals of the white daisies. Tears flooded my eyes, seeing the happy birthday card stuffed in amongst the green stems.

He won't know.

I won't tell him.

I'll do whatever it takes to fix this—and lie, make up some excuse to get rid of Shayne.

Jeremy was sweet enough to let me lie. I know it.

I pulled the card out and flipped it over, then fell to my knees—a quiet but slightly hysterical laugh pushed me over the edge as I read the card, over and over, rubbing the blur from my eyes to make sure it was what it was.

"Andy, are you alright?"

And I let the tears run again—this time for a different reason than expected. I turned, looking up at the beautiful half-naked man, the strong curve of his hips drawn down, half tucked into the towel he wore as he walked towards me.

"You did this?" Just mere moments ago, I had dreamt of how to push him away.

His mouth curled sweetly to one side, eyes widened, that strange darkness haunting his face. "You don't like it."

"Oh my... no," I whimpered, wiping the tear from my eyes, "I love them but how did you know? How did you do this?"

"My first answer is Google." He laughed, rubbing a hand over his chin. "Anyone who puts themselves out there on the web is searchable...all of your little secrets ripe for the picking."

"True," I said, relaxing and a bit relieved that he's not a creep that stole into my room and snooped through my stuff while I wasn't looking.

"And two?"

He grinned, rubbing the towel in his hand over his hair, then draped it over his shoulders. "These are my hotels. I know everything that goes on in them. Like a God of sorts." He gave a quick chuckle. "And, well...I asked the front desk to do it for me."

I didn't know what to say.

All I could do was feel.

No one had ever made this big of a deal over me. No one.

Why does it take a total stranger to make me see that I am allowed to feel like I'm worth loving?

"Who are you?" I said, unable to breathe, feeling my insides shatter. All the pieces of a puzzle that I couldn't find before, now gifted to me by him. Letting myself come undone for just a moment more, realizing I was in trouble, realizing it took a stranger to save me from myself.

"If I would have known that a gift would upset you so much, I would have just bought you a cake."

"I'm not unhappy. It's just that I have never gotten flowers before."

"For your birthday?" He quizzed, his brows raised.

"Ever."

His face blanked, his voice grew hoarse and his hands trembled, just for a minute. "Well, then you are going to hate what's in the box," he said, setting down on the edge of the bed.

"What? Why?"

His hand lifted, gesturing for me to open it. I turned and reached for the box, pulling it open slowly, giving him the evil eye as I pulled it free from the shiny paper. My breath caught as my hand reached in and felt the softness of the silky texture inside.

His eyes narrowed, never leaving mine, watching—evaluating my reaction. I lifted it gently and let the edges of it fall, revealing the soft sheer cuts in the sky coloured blue cloth, delicately embroidered by white lacy flowers.

It was breathtaking.

Clutching it to my chest, I held it tight as I stood motionless, still tucked within the robe.

"If you don't like it..."

"It's beautiful, thank you."

"Well then..." Shayne said, sliding off the bed and to his feet. He dipped his fingers delicately under the fabric, taking it from me, and reached for my hand, pulling me to my feet, "Shall we see how it looks on you?"

Setting the dress on the bed, his hands lowered and tugged the knot loose from my robe, and pulled the edges open. Leaning in he kissed the dip in my collarbone and slid the robe from my shoulders, letting it drop to the floor. Gathering the light blue dress into his hands, he whispered, "Lift your arms."

I raised my hands over my head. He bunched the material together and held it over me then slid it down over my arms. It fell loosely down over my hands, over my head and settled onto the tips of my erected nipples. He leaned down and licked each one before pulling the hem of the dress down over them.

My stomach tightened and my eyes drew shut, the touch of Shayne's tongue setting wild butterflies to take flight underneath the cloth. Slipping the dress over the fullness of my breast, he tugged it down around the curve of my hips then grazed his teeth over his bottom lip.

Watching me with raised brows, catching my strange gaze he laughed. "The blue suits you well."

His hands slowly lowered and draped across my backside as he pulled me into him, hardening again and whispered, "Gaud Miss Morrison, you're dangerously beautiful."

His hot breath made my legs weak, and me to fall into him. He only laughed and gently bit my neck. "Let's eat something before you are the death of me."

He let me go, still lost in him, and turned away, wandering off around the corner. "We can't be doing that stuff all day long on an empty stomach, Miss Morrison. Take the dress off and come eat."

I exhaled, hearing the crinkling of paper bags. Pulling the dress over my head, I slipped back into my robe—stomach growling as I followed the smell of fish n chips.

Chapter 21

We laid quietly on the bed, still as night, and completely full of food. I could hear the sound of Shayne's heartbeat as I rested my head on his chest, while he stroked my hair. Too full to fool around, too tired from fooling around to try, so we remained still in peaceful silence—listening to the sounds of the city and watching the curtains sway against the harbour's breeze as it danced in through the open patio doors.

My eyes grew heavier the longer we laid there, breath grew slow in my contentment.

Just for one minute.

I needed to close my eyes just for a second.

My head jerked, eyes fluttering to stay open as I stared over my bed at the emptiness where I last looked upon Shayne, only to find a note.

"Shayne?" I called out to no reply.

I turned over the note. A flower plucked from the bouquet placed underneath it. Gathering the flower up, I flipped the paper over and read the inscription.

Dinner tonight.
Wear the dress.
A car will pick you up at the door at 8.
Don't be late.
S.M.

I laughed out loud. "Why does he keep doing that?"

Chapter 22

I entered out into the city air, weaving through the rest of the conventioneers, still wandering around the hotel parking lot—done for the day and left to their own devices for entertainment.

Not recognizing anyone, I strode through the spinning doors spying a black Rolls Royce, a tall young man patiently waited by the door.

My eyes narrowed as my stride slowed.

"This can't the car." I breathed out to no one until I heard my name called and a smile grew on the young man's mouth as he approached. "Miss Morrison?"

I smiled back at him and nodded.

"Right this way, Miss." He politely guided me to the back door of the car and opened it, waiting until I climbed in before shutting it behind me. A bucket of ice with a bottle of champagne tucked inside greeted me, another note slipped onto the side of the bucket.

'A drink before dinner?'

Was all that was written in black. I laughed as held the note to my chest just as the window in front of me slid down, and a smiling young man turned to peek over his shoulder at me.

"Good evening, Miss Morrison. Mr. Matthew's asked me to take you on tour of the city before heading to the restaurant. The champagne is to keep you company until he can meet you there later."

"Thank you," I said, pausing to ask for his name.

"Mark," he answered, his mouth curled upward turning back around in his seat to start our tour.

"Thank you, Mark. So, where are we going?"

"Signal Hill, Miss, from up there you can see the whole city."

He wasn't lying.

From the tallest point of the hill, the city of Saint Johns sparkled like little diamonds as the night set in. It was breathtaking.

I stepped out of the car and let the ocean breeze sweep through my hair—the coolness in it clearing my head a bit from the champagne. I'm not sure how long I stood there, staring over the picturesque scene but the crunching gravel of footsteps drew me back to reality as Mark finally made his way over to where I was.

"Sorry, Miss, but we should start back. I was told to have you at the restaurant by nine."

"Oh, no, that's okay," I hummed turning away from the city, "This was lovely, thank you for taking me."

"Don't thank me, thank Mr. Matthew's, it was his idea."
He strode by my side back to the car and opened the door."

"Well, Mark, thank you anyway. It's a beautiful place you live in."

His face flushed just a hint of rose and he bowed his head. "You're quite welcome, miss." He turned around and looked out of the city himself. "And yes ma'am. It's easy to lose yourself here."

It was.

There was something magical about this place but I just couldn't put my finger on. Something so inviting and captivating that I grew a bit sad thinking that in less than twelve hours I would be headed to the airport and flying back to the real life I left behind.

Taking one last look out over the bay, I soaked in as much of this magic as I could before slipping back into the car and heading off towards Mr. Matthews.

Chapter 23

The Maître de seated me in a quiet corner table set for two. Candles lit the space, casting a romantic glow throughout the room. "Can I get you anything to drink while you wait, Miss?"

"Oh, hm, maybe a Rye and ginger would be nice. Thank you," I said smiling at the lovely older lady, hair graced with greys and silvers, enhancing the beautiful space around her.

"Of course, Miss," she chimed, rushing off to get my drink.

I turned and gazed out the window, overlooking the city, watching people pass by on their way home. Lovers strolled through the streets, hand in hand, laughing and holding each other close.

The beautiful woman returned and set my small-glassed drink in front of me, insisting she would return momentarily. My fingers ran down the side of my glass, replaying images of Shayne, and our time together, reliving some of the more intimate moments—the heat of them flushed over my face as I daydreamed.

I sipped at the drink and took in the beautiful room, glancing towards the door now and again to see if my date had arrived yet. But only the waitress was in view at the hostess desk, the phone in her hands as she glanced my way.

Nodding and writing something down, she hung up the phone and started towards my direction with a quiet smile on her face.

"Miss Morrison?"

"Yes?"

"Um, I'm sorry but Mr. Matthews just called and is unable to make it to dinner. He said for you to order anything you like on the menu and that he's sorry."

"Oh," I whispered, suddenly losing my appetite, my stomach dipped, "no, that's alright."

"Are you sure you won't have anything?" The smile on her face was sweet but laced with sympathy.

"No, that's fine," I said trying to hide my disappointment from showing on my face. "I'm not really that hungry anyway."

"Well take your time finishing your drink, and if you change your mind, just give me a wave and I will come right back."

"Thank you," I whispered quietly, granting the girl a forced smile and watched her walk away.

I turned to the window and stared out into the night.

"Oh well."

Tipping back the drink, I set it down then gathered my things to leave. I strode out the front door feeling the evening breeze cooling the heat in my face—the embarrassment stinging about being stood up.

I shouldn't be so upset. He's a multi-million dollar conglomerate owner with a lot on his plate. He probably just got hung up doing business. I can't be mad at him for that.

Mark jumped to his feet from the side of the black rolls still faithfully parked outside the restaurant in waiting. "Finished so soon?"

"Yes, change in plans it seems."

"That tends to happen sometime, doesn't it?" he hummed, a smile still in his eyes. "Shall I drive you home then, Miss?"

A warm breeze fluffed the loose strands of my hair, tickling my neck with is delightful beckoning.

"How far is my hotel from here?"

He glanced over his shoulder and turned back. "It's only a couple streets down then to the left."

"You know what," I hummed, looking beyond him, "I think I'll walk back. The air is warm tonight and it's my last night here so I think I get back on my own. But, thank you, Mark."

"You're sure, Miss?"

"Yes quite, have a good night."

"Yes, Miss," he said closing the back door of the car and walking around to the other side, getting in.

I crossed the road and wandered down the hill toward the hotel. The air was warm tonight truly, much warmer than it had been since I landed. I slowly strolled by the small cafes and the little pubs, open for business, and loud with the sound of people out enjoying the night like myself, peering in on them as I passed by.

I smiled watching all the faces changing as they chatted and told stories over beer or coffee. Turning my head to observe the other side of the street, I stopped quickly. So quickly, I nearly tripped over my own feet. Rushing to the other side of the street, stealing away behind a door that just opened, I gasped for breath—my heart twisting in my chest.

Pressing my eyes shut, I looked away not wanting to believe what I saw—more like not wanting to believe whom it was I saw.

Hands were nestled into Shayne's dark sandy coloured curls, a more delicate hand cupped against his jaw. His head bent into her skin and his eyes closed as their forehead met. Super blond, exotically beautiful with tanned skin, the woman wore earrings that hung from her perfect lobes, and dangled over the black spaghetti straps of her dress. Her other arm hidden—draped around his lower back as she sunk into him, and he into her.

I pulled my eyes away, unable to breathe or to think straight with my heart beating so loudly in my ears.

The very sight of it burning my eyes.

I felt like I was going to be sick. Pushing back the pub door, I ran down the hill—hand covering my mouth, and tucked into the next road—running until I found the street that would lead me back to my hotel.

Back to the place that I never should have left in the first place.

The broad building came into view, hovering over the space like a sleeping giant and I hurried towards it. Tripping over a crack in the sidewalk, I fell into the cement—tearing open my knee, ripping the seam of my beautiful blue dress.

I just sat there in the middle of the lot, tucked up against the tire of a red Camaro, unable to move paralyzed by my sadness.

Damn him and his lies.

Damn him and his stupid presents.

How stupid was I to think any of this was real?

Finally I got up off the ground and I wiped away the tears, enough to see where I was going, and shuffled myself into the back of the hotel—limping from the pain in my knee. Slipping through the back door, I took the stairs up onto the second floor avoiding the lobby altogether. If I looked even half as horrible as I felt, hurting and covered in blood, I would have to answer questions to people I didn't want to see.

I snuck onto the second floor and rushed to the elevator pressing the button repeatedly, praying no one would come out of their rooms until I was gone. With a ding, the door opened and I rushed inside—pressing the close button first, then the top floor.

Leaning face first onto the glass, the waterworks started again.

Why did I let myself do this?

What on earth possessed me to do any of this?

None of this was me—none of it.

And now, I've done so many out of character things...too many things to go back to my old life—at least to the way it was.

Doors opened with a ding.

Pushing away from the glass, I led myself down the hallway—towards the Marilyn suit and opened my door.

Digging around the bathroom, finding a first aid kit under the sink in the bathroom, I rinsed away the dirt and gravel from my knee, patching it up with some alcohol—some for me from the mini-bar and some for the wound.

I stood, looking at myself in the mirror. The girl that looked back at me was no longer able to have happy thoughts. Her eyes danced over the delicate laced flowers of the dress she wore and cringed. I tore at the blue dress, pulling it up over my head and threw it into the trash where it belonged.

Where I felt I belonged.

Pulling on the robe hanging from the bathroom door, shutting off the lights, I hid my face in the darkness—not able to stomach looking at myself any longer.

I drew back the covers of my bed and fell inside of them, letting the numbness take over where the sadness had been. "Just go to sleep Andy," I said to myself, ready to leave this night behind me and move forward. There isn't anything for me here. "It will be over tomorrow."

Closing my eyes, I let the night drift away, and buried everything into the shadows.

Chapter 24

The phone rang out loudly beside my head, jarring me from a restless night. "Hello?" I croaked out.

"This is room service with your seven o'clock wake up call."

"Thank you," I managed to say, my throat still tendered from crying all night. Hanging up the phone, dragging my pathetic self out of bed I stumbled towards the shower. Grabbing the flowers on the way by, I trashed them in the garbage on top of the dress.

Unable to look myself in the eye yet, I kept my eyes low while undressing and stepped into the heat of the shower—letting the rest of my tears wash away down the drain and getting the rest of my pity party out of my system.

It took a good twenty minutes of water therapy to finally sooth me enough to be able to step out. I dried my hair, dressed in my traveling clothes and shut the door of my room, leaving everything behind that wasn't mine.

I handed the keys over to the same sweet girl that had been on duty the day I did my presentation, watching her beam brightly at me, thanking me again, for what I had done for her. I forced a smile and gave her my card—sucking in a deep breath and asking one last time if there were any messages before I left both men behind me.

"No Miss Morrison," she said searching in my room number box then she stopped, "Oh...wait, there is something."

Blood rushed through my veins as she turned and handed me a small envelope—my name written across the top of it in a familiar hand scratch. I took it from her and turned toward the exit, the cab already waiting for me outside as I slipped the small envelope into my coat pocket.

I wasn't ready to read it.

I didn't want to have some kind of last minute break down in front of anyone.

Especially here.

I had shed enough tears here.

I rode all the way to the airport in a quiet state, all of the images of the past two days tearing at my insides but I had to let them.

It was part of my healing. If I kept pushing them away they would only fester and eat at me alive a little bit every day until finally, they would destroy everything I had accomplished so far.

And that was not something I would let happen.

I boarded the plane and settled into my seat, waiting for liftoff. Riffling through my pocket I finally pulled the tiny envelope from it's hiding spot, almost ready to see what it said.

Unfolding the top of it, I pulled out the small piece of paper and exhaled.

Sorry about last night, about everything,
I just couldn't get away. Call me…
S.M.
709-722-9988

I looked away—the site of it scorching my sight. Tears threatened to break down the wall I had started to mend. I looked at it again, letting my eyes slip over the scribbles once more, then crumpled it into my palm and squeezed it hard.

A stewardess dipped into my seat. "Don't forget to buckle your belt miss," she hummed sweetly with a smile then turned to remind the next passenger.

"Oh, um," I squeaked out to her, clenching my fist. "Excuse me."

"Yes?" She turned back and stepped toward me. "Is everything alright?"

"It will be…" I said, holding out my hand, "Would you mind putting this in the garbage for me?"

She held out her hand and I dropped the crumpled note into her cupped fingers.

I watched her as she walked away, carrying with her the last piece that held me to my sins of the past. Then turned away towards the window, and smiled—letting go, forgiving myself, and looking forward to my future.

To continue the journey click here:
https://www.amazon.com/dp/B07RLQT546

To sign up for our newsletter go to https://dl.bookfunnel.com/ps6yp54y7l to get the latest updates and special offers from the author herself.

Or follow her at www.facebook.com/AJMarxAuthor/

Ajmarx.author@gmail.com

Author's Note

First of all thank you so much for reading this book, and sharing the magic of Andy and Shayne's story. If you enjoyed it, I would really appreciate a few words of review on my amazon page. Reviews help other see the book and they help me as an author to get the word out about my writing.

This was an unexpected journey for the three of us (Andy, Shayne and I). I never planned on ever writing this as it wasn't on the schedule at all for this year's writing design.

But as you can see, both Shayne and Andy had other plans for me so who am I to argue, I'm only the scribe that translates for my characters.

I was a little nervous about this project but in the end, I am so glad that I did it. And really hope you enjoy the story as much as I enjoyed the journey of writing it.

Andy and Shayne send along their well wishes and hope to see you at the end of the series.

> With love and gratitude,
> A.J. xoxo
> June, 2019

Books by A.J. Marx

Touch Me Like You Do

Kiss Me Like You Do

Love Me Like You Do

Save Me Like You Do

About the Author - A.J. Marx

A.J. Marx is an incorrigible romantic and huge fan-gal of the written word. After years of working in IT and then a stay-at-home mom, she decided to pursue her next big dream and write stories that readers could fall in love with and really get into. The result is a new and sensuous romance series The Morrison files: Touch Me Like you do, Kiss Me Like you do, Love Me Like you do, and Save Me Like You Do

A.J. Marx is blessed with a beautiful family and lives on the East Coast of New Brunswick, Canada with their Rough Collie, and the neighbourhood deer.